GW01339963

THE DEVIL'S CELLAR

Shane Marco

authorHOUSE®

AuthorHouse™ UK Ltd.
500 Avebury Boulevard
Central Milton Keynes, MK9 2BE
www.authorhouse.co.uk
Phone: 08001974150

This book is a work of fiction. People, places, events, and situations are the product of the author's imagination. Any resemblance to actual persons, living or dead, or historical events, is purely coincidental.

©2011. Shane Marco. All rights reserved.

No part of this book may be reproduced, stored in a retrieval system, or transmitted by any means without the written permission of the author.

First published by AuthorHouse 1/29/2011

ISBN: 978-1-4520-9898-2

This book is printed on acid-free paper.

Foreword

This book is big in volume and smooth while exhibiting great structure, flowing with the luscious fruit flavours of cherries, currants, berries, and plums. On the palate, there is a hint of mocha and herbs, generously framed by toasty English oak. It has a mouth-filling texture, is soft but well structured, and leaves you with an insatiable desire to read more.

The wine is the same. It is dark and deep red in colour made from Merlot and Carménère grapes in the Central Valley region of Chile.

The book follows the path of a bottle of Chilean merlot wine called *Casillero del Diablo* (the Devil's Cellar) as passes, for a multiplicity of reasons, from person to person, with each chapter focusing on another custodian of the wine.

Although the bottle is never opened, the souls of the characters are, and their varying emotions are often spilled.

There are more twists and turns in the novel than there are in a corkscrew.

Sit yourself down in your favourite chair, put on the reading lamp, caress the bottle of *Casillero del Diablo* wine, and try to imagine what secrets it holds. Then open it, pour yourself a glass, and immerse yourself in the trail left by the bottle for you to follow.

But don't forget to wipe it clean of your fingerprints.

Contents

Foreword		v
Preface		vii
Chapter 1.	A Meal for Two	1
Chapter 2.	A Twist of Silk	17
Chapter 3.	No Fury Like a Woman Scorned	31
Chapter 4.	At the End of a Tether	46
Chapter 5.	As Easy as Breathing	60
Chapter 6.	Liver but No Bacon	76
Chapter 7.	An Interview without Coffee	89
Chapter 8.	One Turn Too Many	101
Chapter 9.	Sunset over Blackfriars	113
Chapter 10.	Red and White	128
Chapter 11.	Evens	141
Chapter 12.	Unintended Consequences	156
Chapter 13.	One Club Beats One Heart	170
Chapter 14.	Unconditional Love	183
Epilogue		195

Preface

Detective Inspector Jack Harvey threw a piercing glance at the constable who had had the temerity to try to bar his entrance into the shadowy house that was the scene of the incident. He was loathe to call it a crime until he had checked it himself and reviewed all the forensic evidence. Then, and only then, would he declare it a murder scene—if indeed it was. The two paramedics were sitting on the rear step of the ambulance, holding mugs of a steaming brew poured from a stainless steel flask that rested on the stretcher that had been waiting for the hapless victim. Four police cars were parked randomly across the drive. The incessant flashing of blue lights reflected back from the windows of the adjacent houses, in front of which dozens of onlookers were standing in groups, all theorising as to the events inside 86 Sussex Avenue.

The speculation ranged from a terrorist cell to an escaped lion. Some were right; some concluded that it was a murder. The white polypropylene tape with "Police Incident—Keep Out" printed in blue was joined from lamppost to lamppost with constables placed at intervals along its length. The tape ensured that the growing throng of onlookers did, indeed, keep out. Jack Harvey's car, and the van that had brought the two scene of crime officers, completed the cluster of vehicles. An officer dressed in white overalls met DI Harvey at the front door. Jack raised his eyebrows inquisitively, waiting for the full, concise report from Sgt Harry Cole.

"White male. Dead in his chair; possibly asleep at the time of the attack. Entry through unlocked kitchen door. Happened during the hour that his housekeeper was out. Single blow to the head from behind, probably done by a left-hander judging by the angle; the weapon was most likely a full bottle of wine that we found on the floor, broken in only two pieces. Top still sealed. A few fragments embedded in the victim's scalp; a few splinters on the floor and maybe a few on the attacker somewhere. It looks like there may be some good sets of prints on the bottle. Not that it's relevant, but it was a red wine, a Chilean merlot called *Casillero del Diablo*. We'll wait and see what we can find back in the lab."

Jack grunted his thanks and walked thoughtfully into the lounge, where the victim was sitting in a brown leather club chair, with his head slumped onto his chest as if he had fallen into a deep sleep. The blood patch on the back of the skull had congealed, and the hair was matted, with the signs of the spilled wine evident on the back of the chair. The white shirt was still wet, clinging to the dead man's shoulders and neck, and glass splinters glinted in the drying pool of wine on the polished wooden floor. The housekeeper was in the kitchen with an officer, staring at an imaginary spot on the opposite wall. Jack Harvey wandered from room to room, watching as various officers scurried around, taking photos and fingerprints, looking in cupboards and drawers, checking behind curtains and under beds.

On his way out of the house, Jack took Harry Cole aside and told him to get the evidence to him immediately it became available. He wanted this one solved quickly.

A Meal for Two

"Guv, we've got something." Sgt Terry Price burst into the DI's office without knocking, triumphantly throwing a buff folder onto the desk.

Jack Harvey swung his chair around to face him. "Who've we got, Terry? Take me through it."

Terry leaned over the desk and excitedly opened the file, pointing at the front page. "First set of fingerprints that we've lifted from the bottle, guv. Victor Meredith; he knocked over and killed a kiddie whilst he was drunk. Banned for two years; prison for nine months."

"Do you think he was capable of smashing the bottle of wine over his head? Well?"

"I don't know, guv; have a read, see what you think."

"I will, but find him and get him in for a chat."

Shane Marco

My world was waking. Front doors were being slammed shut, cars were being coaxed into life by overzealous twists of keys, and dogs were barking as they chased their masters along the road. It was 6.57 a.m. I kicked off the duvet to expose my naked body to the chill in the air and swung my legs out of the bed, treading carefully on the growing pile of worn clothes on the floor. The clock was about to shriek at me as I reached across to pre-empt the event. I pressed out two paracetamol tablets from the pack on my bedside table and swallowed them effortlessly, with the help of some gathered saliva, in the hope of easing my still pounding head. I opened the underwear drawer, grabbed a pair of pants and a pair of rolled-up socks, took the seven steps into the bathroom, and nudged up to the toilet for my fifth wee since the previous night. The whoosh of water cleansing the bowl was always my morning reveille, and my eyelids lifted as I greeted Friday. Daylight lit the room; the dull grey light of late summer, or was it early autumn?

I turned toward the basin, rested both hands on the edge, and stared at myself in the mirror. To shave or not to shave, that is the question—smirking at myself for the witty play on words, as if I had never heard them before. I said them most mornings. I rubbed my hand around my face, feeling the stubble, and made the executive decision not to rasp my face that morning. Executive decision indeed! That would be my first, and probably the hardest, of the day.

Droplets of cold water fell onto my bare chest as I splashed my face and, almost subconsciously, scrubbed my hands and nails whilst I gave my tired face a hard look. *Not bad looking, Vic*, I thought, but at the same time, I noticed that the bags around my eyes were dark, hanging, and heavy that morning. I threw another handful of water onto my face, hoping that the cold would tighten the flesh; I peered long and hard, but no reaction. A generous squeeze of toothpaste on the brush and some vigorous brushing soon took away the stale taste in my mouth. A quick rinse and I was done.

I continued staring; I've not really lived, but my face has. Not smoked, avoided drugs, and never been drunk; well, not since that fateful day—the day my sleepless nights started. I always wondered what it would be like to fall into a drunken sleep again—to eventually wake with a hangover—but alcohol had been on the forbidden list since *that* day. Maybe it was time to face my demon. Friday. The thought stayed with me as I continued to gaze at myself. Tonight my colleagues would go out for a drink after work. Mind you, they did this on Thursdays, Wednesdays, Tuesdays, and, I think, on Mondays too, but they had long since stopped asking me to join them. Tonight I would go with them, whether they invited me or not. Yes, tonight the demon dies.

They were a good bunch, sometimes acting in a slightly immature manner but dedicated to the company. Most had been there since the day that the business had been started some four years earlier. The term *young executive* had worn thin, but at least I had my own office on the third floor with a personal assistant, Alison, and I did a useful job of pulling together the sales department on the upper floors and the assembly plant downstairs.

All day, my mind was on how I was about to succumb to alcohol that night, and during our lunch break in the canteen, I announced that I was going to join them in the pub that evening. One of the guys looked around shiftily and said in a conspiratorially subdued way, "We actually go to bars these days, Vic."

The day was drawing to a close with the farewells and whoops of delight ringing in the air. I turned off my computer, neatened my desk, pulled the blinds, and said good night to Alison. I checked that my car keys were in my pocket and announced to anyone who wanted to listen, "Who wants a lift?" The silence was deafening. I looked around enquiringly.

"Vic," said Darren, "we daren't drive—we get cabs!"

Ah, I thought. "So tell me where we are going then, and I'll drop the car home and get a cab."

"Belle Aire, Hounsden Street," came the resounding reply from at least five of my colleagues.

"See you all later," I called back as I walked through the corridor to the rear staircase, which took me down to the car park where my black Mini Cooper stood alone in the reserved space near the exit. The engine burst into life, and as I settled into the seat and fastened the seat belt, the radio blared with the end of the first verse of my favourite song: *"Satan laughing with delight the day the music died."* After all the years, I could still remember all the words—but not necessarily in the right order.

Why on earth am I considering going out to get drunk? I muttered to myself. *Get a grip on reality, Vic!* I turned off the radio and drove in silence for a few minutes. Just ahead was a supermarket. Indicating left, I pulled into the store's car park and began to sing more lines from *"American Pie."*

The doors opened automatically, and as I entered the store, I was greeted by an assistant offering me a nibble of cheese. I wandered up and down the aisles, with the taste of the

The Devil's Cellar

cheese lingering, looking for inspiration. I could not decide; I was not in the mood for a salad. Should it be a baguette and pâté or a meat pie? The chiller section at the back of the store offered a choice of meals-for-one. Decisions, decisions! The spaghetti Bolognese with a separate sachet of Parmesan got my vote. Aiming toward the express checkout, passing feminine hygiene and biscuits and cakes, I came to the wine section. I paused. The thoughts of a drunken stupor and the promise of a full night's sleep persuaded me to stop. I looked at the array of wines on offer. White, red, rosé, Champagnes, New World, French, German, Italian … I looked up and down, from side to side, until my eyes were caught by a bottle with an evocative name—*Casillero del Diablo—Merlot 2006*. I picked up the bottle to read the label on the back. Small lettering takes no prisoners when it comes to failing eyesight.

An arm reached out and grasped a similar bottle of the merlot from the shelf. I looked at the red manicured nails on the fingers of the hand that lowered the bottle into her basket. "This goes well with spaghetti Bolognese," she said.

I looked up; our eyes locked for the briefest of moments. I mumbled a thank you and looked down at the label again. In that short space of time, I had inhaled all of her.

She was my sort of age, with hair falling on her shoulders, either expensively cut or naturally tidy—I never was any good at deciphering which. She wore a red V-neck sweater with the sleeves pulled up to the forearm, with the hem of the jumper resting on her hips over a straight black skirt. She was still standing there as I moved my eyes sideways, keeping my head motionless, in order to look at her shapely legs and matching red shoes. I wanted to look back to her face but I felt uncharacteristically shy. I got as far as her basket containing a meal-for-one and the merlot. And the wedding ring.

I got to the Hand Baskets Only queue just as the previous customer was paying. I took the two items from my basket and put them on the conveyor belt, placing the next-customer divider after my goods. As I dropped the empty basket into the rack, I saw her behind me in the queue. This time I looked at her and said, "Hi again."

She smiled and was just about to say something when the young cashier said, "These are two for the price of one," holding up the wine.

I turned back to her, excused myself, took her bottle from the conveyor, and placed it next to mine. The second bottle was scanned and the boy pulled my meal-for-one through the scanner. "These are two for one too, sir," he said.

As if I had been doing it for years, I reached back, took her meal-for-one, and gave it to the cashier with a smirk. She stood there totally unfazed by it all, with the hint of a smile on her lips. I paid the cashier with a £10 note and dropped the change into a conveniently placed charity box by the wall. I put her items and mine in separate bags and walked toward the exit with her by my side.

"That was quick thinking," she said.

She proffered a five-pound note at me but I shook my head dismissively.

"Thank you, kind sir," she said as she reached for the bag nearest her.

The Devil's Cellar

I hung onto it as I said, "Why don't you buy a lottery ticket?"

"No point" she replied with a dismissive wave of her hand.

"Go on," I said, "we can always give our winnings to charity."

She peeled away from me and walked purposefully toward the lottery kiosk.

"£5 Lucky Dip, please, for tomorrow." The cashier exchanged the note for a ticket, which she slipped into the carrier bag that I held out to her.

"Where's your car?" I asked, and she pointed in a vague 'over there' direction. We walked a few paces before I introduced myself. "My name is Victor; call me Vic."

"Hello, Victor," she replied and then paused before adding, "I prefer Victor."

I waited for hers—she stayed silent.

Five paces later, she said, "Here's my car," pointing to a black Mini Cooper parked nose to nose with mine. I passed the bag to her as she clicked her key fob to unlock her car. I had done the same thing, and both cars winked their lights at each other. She smiled with her full red lips. And with her eyes too.

"Victor, as this was two for the price of one, will you join me for supper? Two meals cook as easily as one."

My smile said it all.

"Follow me," she said as she closed her door, slipped the car into gear, and drove toward the exit.

I was at least thirty seconds behind her and smiled as I saw her car in the lay-by waiting. It was only a five-minute drive to her home, which was in a quiet block of apartments at the end of a cul-de-sac. I took the bag from her as she led me to the second floor, where she opened the door of her flat, pushing a pile of letters and junk mail away from the threshold. I bent down and picked them up. "Mrs T. Reynolds," it said on one of the envelopes.

"What does the 'T' stand for?" I asked.

"Tess," she replied.

"Short for Tessa?" I asked.

"No, just Tess."

The short corridor led to a spacious and bright (as the agents would say) living room, tastefully furnished and decorated in beech wood and black leather. "I *must* have a shower," she said as she kicked off her shoes. "You will find a corkscrew in the third drawer in the kitchen and some wine glasses in the cupboard above. I won't be long."

I unpacked our dinner, putting the two meals by the side of the microwave and one bottle of wine in the corner by the fridge; I placed the lotto ticket under the bottle for safekeeping. The drawer contained a few instruction manuals for her appliances, three packs of strong painkillers, and the promised corkscrew still bearing the spoils of its last excursion. Slowly untwisting the old cork, I took out the other bottle from the bag, peeled off the foil, and with

The Devil's Cellar

long forgotten skills, pulled the cork. I took two glasses and poured the rich red wine, with the customary and comforting glug, into the goblets.

I opened the fridge quietly, not wishing my spying to be heard, and found inside some milk, eggs, low fat spread, and some bits of salad ingredients. I walked toward the bathroom, with the intention of asking through the door if I should make a salad. As I got closer, I heard the sounds of Don McLean's *"American Pie"* resonating from behind the door, muffled slightly by the sound of the water pouring from the showerhead, yet enhanced by Tess singing along tunefully.

"This'll be the day that I die..."

I flushed at the thought of her standing naked just a few feet away from me; my hand was just a few centimetres away from the door handle. I shook the notion out of my mind and went back to the lounge, singing the infectious song, and sat on one of the two armchairs. My thoughts were in overdrive, and no matter how hard I tried, the image of Tess in the shower stayed with me until I saw an old leather-bound, gold-leafed, book on the coffee table. I picked it up. *Tess of the d'Urbervilles* by Thomas Hardy. The inside cover was inscribed "To *MY* Tess—all my love, Derek." Derek, who the hell is Derek? Her husband?

She walked in. I looked up and involuntarily held my breath as I stood to greet her. She looked strikingly glamorous. Her colour scheme was the same, but now she was wearing a black V-neck jumper, a red skirt, and black shoes, and her legs sheathed in black nylon. Black and red were certainly her colours, and she knew how to use them to the best advantage—the little devil!

"I was going to ask if I should make us a salad," I said nervously.

She replied with a curt nod, softened by one of her smiles. We stood side by side in the kitchen, and as I sliced and chopped the vegetables, she slipped the covers off the two meals-for-one and placed them side by side in the microwave.

The full glasses of wine stood like sentries next to the half-full bottle.

"Ten minutes," she said as she opened the cupboard and took out two dinner plates and two matching side plates. She opened the top drawer and took out two knives and two forks, which she brought to the table together with the smaller plates. I finished making the salad, such as it was. Not a lot could be done with one tomato, a dried-up end of a cucumber, a salvaged onion, and a shrivelled carrot. But, drizzled with some olive oil, it looked passable.

She took the two full wine glasses into the dining area and put them on the table, and then she went back into the kitchen to retrieve the ready-meals. I carried the salad and the bottle, and we sat down to eat. I needed to break through this nervy interaction between us. I told her my age; that I was a director at *Cyclops;* that I had been divorced for eight years; that I had a son at *Leeds University* studying law. She told me that she was a teacher. I told her that I lived in an apartment opposite the park; that my ex-wife had remarried; that my PA was called Alison. She told me that she taught nine-year-olds. Undaunted, I carried on. She listened intently, nodding and smiling. I tried jokes—not my forte—and I almost got a laugh from her at one of them.

The wine glasses remained in front of us, untouched. I declined coffee and stood to leave. Tess stood too, walked purposefully toward me, and kissed me firmly but tenderly on the lips—a moment too long, perhaps, as I returned her kiss with passion, forcing my tongue into her mouth. She pulled away and said, "No—my husband."

"Is he due home?" I asked.

"I wish," she responded, and after a short pause, she added, "He's dead. He died last year—today is the anniversary."

Now I understood. But what should I do? Offer her some sweet tea? A cuddle? Or say, "Do you want to talk about it?" All I managed was a heartfelt "I am so sorry," even though I was elated that she was unattached. She led me to the front door. I fumbled in my pocket for a business card. "If you need me, call me—home number, office switchboard, direct line, e-mail—business and personal; mobile, likewise."

I laughed to myself at the information on the card and thought that maybe it should have my collar size and inside leg measurement on the back. Tess threw me one last smile as she ushered me toward the stairs.

I drove home slowly, singing *"American Pie"* all the way.

I needed no alarm. I woke with my head thumping—not with a headache but with nauseous fear. Why didn't I see it last night? What an idiot I was! I was trying to stay rational, but I couldn't. I felt sick and frantic. I grabbed some clothes from the pile on the floor, pulling them on as I ran to the front door.

I did my belt up at the same time as I released the car door lock, dived into the seat, slammed the gear stick into first, and screeched away with my foot hard on the accelerator.

What a fool, what a stupid, *stupid* man! The clues were there. Her silences; the anniversary of her husband's death; the twenty-four strong painkillers; the bottle of wine. My doctor-friend once told me that twenty of those pills taken with a bottle of wine would be fatal. And her singing, *"This will be the day that I die."* God, *please*. I didn't notice whether the traffic lights were red. The dashboard clock said 6.43 as I turned the engine off outside her flat and ran to the door. My hand hit all of the intercom buzzers and stayed there. I yelled, "It's me," into the microphone to whoever asked, and in only a few seconds I heard the lock click open. I rushed through the door, ran up the two flights of stairs to her flat, and banged on her door, screaming, "Open up, Tess, for God's sake, open up!" I hammered again and again. My stomach churned. No answer—then I heard her from the other side, a shaky voice asking who it was.

"It's me, it's Victor."

The lock turned and the door opened. I couldn't help myself and ejected the previous night's meal-for-one all over her wooden floor. Neither could I avoid her bare feet (with matching red painted toenails—which even in that undignified moment I couldn't help but notice). She took a step back and, without a trace of panic in her voice, said, "Victor, what on earth is the matter?"

"Everything is fine—now," I said, taking deep gulps of air. "Give me a few cloths, some newspapers, and a bucket of water, then go and wash your feet. I'll tell you everything after I clean your floor." I mumbled, looking down at the mess. As I looked up, she turned away and took some cloths and a bucket from an adjacent cupboard. She was wearing a thin red silky dressing gown; her hair flowing as she moved. *Natural*, I thought to myself, *no need for the hairdresser.*

By the time she returned, obviously showered but still wearing the same dressing gown, I had cleaned the floor. I held the bucket outstretched in one hand and my shoes in the other. I knew where the bathroom was and did the best I could in washing out the bucket and wiping my shoes. The door was pushed open, and Tess, standing in the frame, said in a schoolmistress tone, "Victor, put that down, come into the lounge, and tell me what this is all about."

I realised that that sentence was the longest she had spoken since we met. Barefooted, unshaven now for two days, wearing yesterday's clothes (or was it from earlier in the week?); I followed her and sat, shamefaced, in a chair.

She stood facing me. "So?" she asked sternly.

I didn't know where to begin. I blurted it all out to her; she listened intently and then walked toward me, sat on the arm of my chair, kissed my forehead, and whispered, "Thank you for caring." It came from her heart.

"Coffee?" she asked. I nodded.

She came back a few minutes later with two steaming mugs of black coffee. She sat in the opposite chair, quite immodestly, with the gown gaping, revealing a deep cleavage.

"You were almost right," she said after a prolonged silence. "I was, at the very least, going to get drunk on a bottle of Derek's favourite wine" (she confirmed my suspicions).

I laughed. In response to her frown, I told her that I was going to do the same thing.

We laughed together. "And '*American Pie*'?" I asked.

Tess opened her mouth as if to answer, paused, and then closed it again. A few seconds passed before she did speak.

"Can I tell you another time?"

I stood up to leave.

"On one condition" I said, "Can I take you for dinner tonight?"

"That would be lovely." she replied.

Conscious of my vile bile-smelling breath, unshaven and unwashed face and teeth, I took her left hand in mine and kissed it. "Pick you up at eight?" She nodded.

I walked toward the front door, collecting my shoes on the way. "Victor, take your wine."

I stopped and waited as she brought it to me. "Don't lose the lottery ticket—we might win, and that's dinner paid for!"

"It's safe—don't worry," she said, patting the breast pocket on her gown.

My son, James, was coming over for lunch. I bathed and shaved, threw the washing into the machine, and tidied around as best as I could. As usual, he was an hour late. I had hardly seen him during the summer, as he had spent it with his friends on some unpronounceable Greek island. But he was going back to University on Monday, and no doubt, he needed some money. The buzzer sounded, and I pressed the button to release the door lock. He looked great, taller than me, bronzed with gleaming teeth and a broad smile. We gave each other a brief, but meaningful, hug and then walked through to the kitchen, where we sat chatting and eating the sandwiches that I had made earlier. I had promised him a new car that summer. It hadn't happened, and I pledged to remedy that whenever it was convenient for him. He began looking at his watch. "You off, son?" I asked.

In answer, he stood up. "Dad, do you have a spare bottle? I'm going to a party tonight—you know a pre-uni party."

I pointed to the bottle of *Casillero del Diablo*. He picked it up. "The Devil's Cellar—from Chile," he said in an impressed voice. I put that down to his experience with alcohol rather than his knowledge of Spanish or geography. We said our farewells. I wished him a safe journey, telling him to call or text me when he was back in Leeds. Of course, I knew he wouldn't; he never had before.

I was unfashionably early at Tess's. She was unfashionably ready. She was wearing a black button-through dress with a red chiffon scarf around her neck, tucked under the collar, which matched her shoes, lips, and nails. Our lips met in greeting.

We walked a short distance to a popular, but intimate, Italian restaurant. We sat in a quiet corner, and the conversation flowed. We laughed, we smiled, we held hands across the table. We even ate average pasta. We shared an American apple pie. We declined coffee. I had this feeling that *she* and *I* were a *we*.

Shane Marco

Back at her flat, I drifted into the lounge; she went into the kitchen to make coffee. The two full wine glasses, untouched from the previous night, were still on the table, with the bottle standing almost symmetrically between them.

The remote control for the television was on the armchair. Out of habit, I flicked the On button and scrolled through the channels. "Check the lottery." came the voice from the kitchen. I found the channel with the results.

"Bring the ticket with you," I said.

She put the cups on the table between us and started to call the numbers. I wasn't sure how much a line of five paid, but it didn't matter: we won. We celebrated in hugs and kisses, in laughter, and with elation. "A holiday," I proclaimed, looking at the *Casillero del Diablo* that had brought us together; "to Chile."

Tess held my hand and led me to her bedroom. To the Victor, the spoils; I smiled at the thought. She fiddled with her CD player and the haunting strains of Don McLean's *"Vincent"* filled the air. I unbuttoned her dress to reveal a perfect bosom, red suspenders holding up her black stockings, with the tiniest pair of red panties. The red scarf stayed on. *Horny devil,* I thought. She toyed with me, and I with her.

It wasn't long until I entered the Devil's Cellar.

A Twist of Silk

Harry Cole, from forensics, sat down beside Jack Harvey in the staff canteen.

"No luck with Victor Meredith, then, sir?"

Jack put his teacup back on the saucer.

"Nope—solid alibi. Wasn't him. Anyway, he wouldn't have had the stomach for it. Decent chap. Made a mistake and put it behind him. Getting married to a teacher."

"I couldn't find Sgt Price, sir, but we've got another set of prints. I don't have the file, sir, but they match with Victor's son, James."

"Not surprising, I suppose, but I'll get Terry on it right away. Thanks. By the way, how many sets of prints are there?" DI Harvey asked.

"Dozens, sir, the few clear ones are easy; so many overlap. It's a problem, but we are working on it, sir."

Shane Marco

James was home in less than twenty minutes and walked into the house where he had lived with his parents until they had decided to separate. In order to cause as little disruption as possible, Vic moved into a flat, allowing his son and his ex-wife, Sue, to stay in the family home. Sue remarried four years later to Edward, an architect with a full greying beard and leather patches on leather patches on his jackets. James called him "Steady Eddie," but they got on well enough together, sometimes even sharing a pint or two at the local pub. His beard still showed signs of nicotine stains from his habitual sucking on a pipe. Sue had allowed him to continue his vice for exactly two weeks after their wedding. Eddie knew his place. Sue put her cheek out for a kiss from James as he came into the kitchen; Eddie lifted his eyes from his trade journal in acknowledgement.

"And how *is* your father?" Sue asked.

James reached in his pocket and pulled out the cheque that his dad had given him, raising it triumphantly above his head whilst imitating the sound of a bugle fanfare.

"Strange thing though, Mum; Dad made us both sandwiches—with the bread buttered on the outside."

Sue was silent as she cast her mind back to the first time Vic had made her a sandwich—buttered on the outside. *He must be in love*, she thought.

"When are you going back to Leeds?" Eddie asked.

"Monday, I think; we start lectures on Wednesday. We're having a farewell party at Jon's place tonight."

"Jon's poor mum!" Sue mumbled and, raising her voice, added, "Are you going with Danni, son?"

"Yes, Mum, but it may be the end. We're not the same people anymore."

At eight o'clock, James pulled into the spacious driveway of 32 Hamden Avenue (also known as *The Squirrels*) and steered his car to the side. Danni would drive to the party so that he could have a few beers—she hardly ever drank and was happy to be James's chauffeur.

Danni and James had known each other all their school life. As they got older, they became close friends and had become inseparable in their fifth year. She was an aspiring glamour queen; strikingly beautiful with golden hair, a dazzling smile, and a shapely body. She also had a GCSE in Home Economics. He achieved ten GCSEs at grade A and two at grade B. At the end of that school year, Danni left to start work in a local department store whilst James went back to the lower sixth form to study A levels; although they saw each other regularly, the difference in their intellect soon began to put a strain on their relationship. He decided that tonight he would end it. But not till after he had had a few drinks.

James turned off the engine, reached across to the passenger seat to get the wine that his dad had given him, and strolled to the front door. As James was about to ring the bell, the door opened and Danni's father, Stan, stepped out. "See you later," he called over his shoulder, colliding with James and almost knocking the bottle from his grasp.

"Hello, James! How you doing?" he said, almost by way of an apology.

"Go right in; see you later," Stan answered.

James walked into the lounge and called, "Hello? Anyone home?" Veronica, Danni's mother, was deep in thought – dreaming about her tennis coach; young, fit, sexy and tall. Unlike Stan who was anything but and would arrive home drunk and stinking of tobacco. She closed her thoughts on hearing James. Almost.

"Hello, James, lovely to see you. How are you?"

By way of a response, James went over and politely kissed her on the cheek. She was wearing a white tennis skirt, T-shirt, and a pair of sports socks on her feet with navy blue stripes on them. She was still very beautiful and probably *had* been a glamour queen. As she padded across the floor, she left moist footmarks from the damp socks—evidently, she had only just taken off her trainers. "Coffee?" she asked. "I am just going to make myself one."

"Please," he replied; as he moved toward the table, he stared at her shapely thighs. James heard the tap being turned on, followed by a scream as cold water bounced off the side of the sink and splashed up over Veronica. He looked up, and she was standing there soaking wet, with a shocked look on her face. James grabbed a towel and started to pat her face dry. Her T-shirt had become transparent, as was expected in all wet T-shirt competitions. James didn't gasp—he just stared. As she looked at James in the eyes, she guided his hand with the towel to her bosom. James let the towel drop and began kneading her perfect breasts, which had been created by the team at the *London Breast Clinic;* a secret shared between her and her surgeon. She eased James backward to a chair, where the edge of the seat caught the back of his knees. As he sat with a jolt, she sat astride him, lifting both his hands

The Devil's Cellar

to her chest, and then her hands moved down and fumbled for his zip.

She arrived just before him; her glowing face on his shoulder; their breathing became shallower as her pounding heart began to slow. At that moment, the outside security lights came on, illuminating the dark room, and they heard the sound of a car screeching to a halt on the gravel drive. "Danni!" Veronica said with a startled voice. She jumped off James's lap and scampered out of the kitchen and up the stairs.

James did up his trousers and took the few quick steps into the darkened lounge, where he sank into the nearest chair. The front door slammed, and Danni shouted for James; she ran into the lounge and threw herself on him. "Darling, I missed you so much!" She kissed him with passion, and it crossed James's mind that it was fortunate that her mum hadn't been wearing perfume. "Let me get out of these work clothes, have a shower, and we'll be ready to go. I'm *so* excited," she squealed, with a cheeky grin on her face. "Tonight you are all mine!"

They both stood up. James had made up his mind. He realized that he couldn't wait until after the party before he told her. "Danni, it's over."

"What is?" she replied with an incredulous look on her face, not wanting to believe what she was hearing.

"Us," he said, dropping his head in remorse.

There was silence from her. James kissed her forehead and ran to the front door, out of the house, and along the drive to his car. The curtain upstairs pulled aside, and Veronica watched her lover accelerate backward onto the road.

James returned to an empty home and went straight upstairs to his bedroom. He turned the volume on his CD player to full, lay on his bed, and stared at the ceiling as the shadows from the streetlights danced through the leaves of the tree outside his window, creating tantalising shadows that reminded him of Veronica.

He took out his mobile phone from his hip pocket, which, to his mother's annoyance, was invariably set to silent mode, and noticed that he had missed nine calls, seven voice messages, and five text messages—all from Danni.

She was beside herself, sobbing uncontrollably. Veronica did what she could to pacify her daughter but with little success. There was no response from her calls to James, and in frustration, Danni threw her phone onto the settee and ran upstairs, slamming her bedroom door behind her. *She'll get over it*, Veronica thought, and started her night time ritual of tidying up. She picked up Danni's phone and was about to place it next to the bottle of wine that James had left behind. She paused in thought for a moment and then turned on the phone and scrolled through the address book to find James's number. Veronica picked up her own mobile from the counter-top and entered the number. She put on the kettle, taking a mug and a mint tea bag from the cupboard. Stan wouldn't be home from his club for some time.

She smiled as she sat in the chair that she and James had been on just a short time before and pleasured herself as she played the scene over again in her mind.

At breakfast, James announced that he had decided to go back to Leeds that day instead of the next, and with his mother helping him pack, he was ready to leave by two o'clock.

"Erm, can anyone lend me fifty quid? I will need some petrol," James said hesitantly. Sue reached for her bag.

"Put in on your credit card," Eddie said, motioning Sue to close her purse.

James announced that he had no credit left and owed the full £5,000. "What will you do?" Sue asked.

"I'll sort out a student loan in the week," James responded in a carefree manner.

"It'll need repaying," said Eddie.

"First month's salary will sort that out," James responded jauntily.

Eddie tried, and succeeded, in stifling a laugh.

Before nightfall on that Sunday, James was back in Leeds. He noticed more calls that he had missed on his mobile as he phoned around to see if anyone else was back and fancied meeting for a drink.

James woke around midday on Monday after a heavy and enjoyable night's drinking. He noticed the flashing screen on his mobile phone, which had been left on silent all night, showing a number rather than a name from his address book. He chose not to answer the call. When it rang again for the third time, he answered. "Hello?" he said inquisitively.

"James?" came the response. "It's me, Veronica."

He drew a breath and held it.

"I'm coming up to Leeds next weekend," she said. "Can we get together?"

James exhaled and paused for a moment before replying that that would be lovely.

"See you Friday, then, James," she said, and without waiting for a reply, she hung up.

At dinner that night, taken without Danni, who was on a hunger strike, Veronica announced that she was going to Harrogate on the forthcoming weekend to visit her old college friend. She knew Stan wouldn't want to join her, as he didn't much like Jules, and he liked her husband even less.

By Friday, Danni seemed to be over the worst of her ordeal. After breakfast, Veronica said farewell to her and Stan as they left for work. She was looking forward to the drive in her convertible Audi TT; she estimated the trip would take no longer than three hours. By two o'clock, having made a call to Jules to set up an alibi, she was ready to leave. She had made a reservation at the four-star *Crown Hotel* and booked dinner for two at eight. She called James and left a message telling him of the arrangements.

James picked up the message, but he was having second thoughts.

Dressed in jeans, trainers, and a striped jumper, Veronica threw her oversized suitcase in the boot, wedging the bottle of *Casillero del Diablo* behind it so it would remain secure

The Devil's Cellar

for the journey. She set her satellite navigation system for her destination; "Your route is set and is 202 miles and you will arrive at approximately 5.07 p.m.," the synthesised voice announced. She dropped the roof of the car, moved her sunglasses from where they were nestling in her hair onto her nose, moved the lever into first gear, and let the clutch out.

The traffic on the Leeds-to-Harrogate road was slow due to the Friday rush hour traffic. It was almost six o'clock by the time she pulled into the small car park at the front of the hotel. Veronica registered and confirmed her restaurant reservation for two at eight o'clock. She was given her key card to room 323, which was at the front of the hotel on the third floor. If she craned her neck, she could just see the rear of her car below. She sent a text message to James, telling him that she had arrived and he was to meet her in *Henry's Bar* on the ground floor at 7.30.

Veronica rummaged through the suitcase for her toiletries bag, taking out her shampoo and conditioner. She showered first, washing her shoulder-length hair twice, and then put in the plug to allow the bath to fill. She reached for the complimentary bottle of bubbles and poured it into the water, lowered herself into the tub, and let the water from the showerhead splash on her shins.

Aware of the time, and before the water had even reached the overflow outlet, Veronica pulled herself up, turned off all the taps, stepped out of the bath, and wrapped herself in a soft towel. By 7.22, she was nearly ready to take the lift to the ground floor. She had dressed in a black calf-length skirt covering black lace-top hold-ups. Her simple shirt was black cotton, and she wore, in college style, a black silk scarf that complemented her shiny black patent leather high-heeled boots.

She wore nothing else.

Veronica quickly tidied the room; she picked up her phone, room card, and small black clutch bag; and with a final flourish, she placed the bottle of *Casillero del Diablo* on the bedside table together with two glasses and the corkscrew conveniently provided by the hotel.

As soon as she sat in the bar at a table facing the entrance, a waiter approached to take her order. The double vodka and tonic (ice, but no lemon) was set before her at 7.30 precisely. At 7.40, after she had ordered a second drink, she telephoned James. Again she left a message. James was in the Student's Union playing out the best of five at the pool table. His phone was in his back pocket and, as usual, switched to silent. He had made his mind up and decided not to meet with Veronica. He felt bad that he would be letting her down, but in any case, he hadn't finished his game of pool or his pint.

Veronica's third and fourth drinks arrived in quick succession as she tried several more times to reach James, without luck. By eight o'clock, she was conscious of a man sitting two tables away who glanced at her from time to time. He had a rugged face with a pronounced scar flowing from the middle of his forehead in a curve toward his right ear, across his cheek, and finishing at the corner of his mouth.

When the waiter brought her fifth drink, she asked for the bill and told him to cancel her dinner reservation. Veronica signed the account, and as the waiter moved aside, her eyes met the stranger's—and locked. After a few moments, he

The Devil's Cellar

stood up and, without breaking the stare, walked the few paces to her table, leaving his half-finished glass of beer. He was tall and, like her, wearing all black.

"Your room or mine?" he said in a slight accent that Veronica could not identify. Had she been more sober, she would have recognised it as southern Irish.

She stood and walked beside him to the lift. In response, she held her room card in front of her at shoulder level. Lucky for him, since he did not have a room in the hotel. No words were exchanged. He was tall, maybe by a clear twelve inches more than she was. As the lift doors closed, he put his hands behind her, grasped her buttocks, and effortlessly lifted her so that they were nose to nose. He roughly kissed her hard and deep, a kiss that lasted the journey to the third floor, a kiss that she returned with passion. As her excitement mounted, she wondered if he was built in proportion to his height. The key card operated the lock on the first attempt. She pushed the door open, and they stumbled into the room, which was in darkness except for the light from the street that glimmered through the chinked curtain.

Veronica had removed her skirt, blouse, and boots before he had dropped his second boot. At 8.14, he rolled on top of her, entering her without any preliminaries. She gasped initially in pain, then, in pleasure—he *was* in proportion. At 8.21, he rolled off. They played for another hour or so, he pleasing her and then her pleasing him. At 9.15, she fell into a deep sleep; he slept too, but restlessly.

Ten hours later, he woke. She hadn't. He rolled on top of her and entered her violently; she woke with a start but her eyes stayed closed so she could focus all of her senses. As his hips began to move faster, he reached for her scarf, looping it around her neck and tying it in a loose knot. She sighed in pleasure. He wrapped each end of the scarf around his hands and began to pull. She was pinned down under his weight as he pulled the scarf tighter whilst he continued his thrusting. She gasped for breath; her eyes were now wide open and staring as she realised, in horror, what was happening to her. Under any other circumstances, she would have noticed the red, black, and yellow tattoo of the devil on his chest. As she took her last breath, he deposited his DNA sample inside her. It was 7.27. The man in black was trained to kill. And he enjoyed it.

Unhurriedly, he showered and dressed, and then tipped the contents of her bag onto the dresser, putting the money, including her small change, into his pocket, together with the keys to the Audi. He left her credit cards. He looked around one final time and noticed the unopened bottle of *Casillero del Diablo*. He took that too. The man in black walked down the three flights of stairs into the lobby, past the unattended reception desk, and through the revolving doors. The lights of her car flashed in response to him pressing the remote control key fob. He slid back the seat to its limit, drove into the traffic, and headed toward Leeds on the A61. It was 7.55.

At 8.40, he parked the car in a quiet street in the centre of town. He took the bottle of wine from the passenger seat, locked the car, tossed the keys into the bushes, and made the short walk to *Mario's Café*. He picked up a *Daily Mirror* from the counter on his way to a table near the back. The full English breakfast with three mugs of tea and extra toast was paid for with the money he had taken from Veronica's bag.

At 9.26, he left the café, clutching the paper. He mistakenly left the wine bottle on the table as if it were part of the cruet.

At 9.28, Magda cleared the table and took the bottle of wine to the cloakroom, where she put it in her shopping bag. Her man would have that with their meal tonight, she decided.

At 9.50, the man in black arrived at his basement squat.

At 11.32, Carol knocked on the door of room 323 of the *Crown Hotel*. "Housekeeping," she announced. As there was no response, she slipped her master key card into the lock, wedged the door open and went to retrieve her trolley from outside the last serviced room.

At 11.33, Carol screamed.

At 1.46, two uniformed police officers knocked on the door of *The Squirrels*. One minute later, Danni and Stan collapsed in shock into each other's arms.

At 2.35, twelve police officers, some of them armed, all of them in protective vests, broke down the door of James's room. He was cautioned, handcuffed, and taken to the police station for questioning, leaving a team of forensic investigators behind.

The three o'clock news on the radio announced that a forty-year-old woman had been found dead in a hotel in Yorkshire and that the police had arrested a man in connection with the murder.

On the four o'clock news, they announced that he had been released without charge.

Back in the squat, the man in black put his few possessions

in a small bag and slung it across his shoulder. He tore up some newspapers and piled them on the sleeping bag that had been his bed for nearly a year since he had been discharged from the army. He poured some paraffin from the lamp that had been his only source of light onto the paper, lit a match, and watched for a few seconds as it blazed alight.

At 4.36, the devil left his cellar.

No Fury Like a Woman Scorned

Jack was standing with both his hands in his trouser pockets, gazing through the open window. It was a warm day, and he was looking forward to a few days off from work. On hearing the knock on the door, he turned. Sgt Price came in. "So, it wasn't James then?" DI Harvey said in a dejected voice, having read Terry's report.

"No, guv, he was out of the country. Anyway, he is an innocent lad, just got caught up in a nasty incident. That enquiry is still open, guv. I wonder if there *is* a connection."

"Not our problem, Terry, it's with the Leeds force. What bemuses me is that there appears to be no motive. They are always the hardest to clear up. The profile of the victim was a good piece of work. Who did it?"

"It was a new WPC, Geraldine Ennin. Fresh out of Hendon. Bright girl."

"Anything else, Terry?"

"Yes, guv, a set of prints from an ex-pro and porn artiste, Rosalind Tomkins. She was in television but we're having a few problems tracing her."

"And so it's good night from me, Zoe Zealand, the producer, and entire production team. We will be back next year. Until then …"

"And wrap!" said Gordon. The last episode had been recorded and was ready for editing prior to the nationwide broadcast two days later.

Zoe stood up to applause from the cameramen and stage crew. She smiled, took a bow, and left through the swinging doors. The gang clapped and backslapped each other before slowly moving on to the business of closing down the studio for the night, whilst still in animated conversation. Gordon went back into the control room and turned on the speaker: "All of you up to the office for celebrations when you're done."

Sara, Gordon's personal assistant, had arranged food and drinks for the team and was waiting on Mario to make the delivery. She looked at her watch yet again, concerned that the food hadn't arrived.

"'ello, Mario's. Can I 'elp you?" Although Mario was a second-generation Italian immigrant, he spoke as if he had just arrived in England from Naples.

"Hi, Mario, it's Sara from the Studios—is our food on its way?"

"Be wiv you in five minutes, *mia caro*; *ciao*." He called to

Magda, who was in the kitchen, to ask if the Studio's order was ready.

"Just putting the platters in the trolley—how many wines was it, Mario?"

Mario checked the order. "Three red and three white—they are in the cupboard."

Magda moved the chair from in front of the door to the store cupboard and pulled the box of wines toward her. The café was unlicensed but Mario always held a private supply for corporate customers.

"One red short, Mario!" shouted Magda. As the words left her lips, she remembered the bottle from the table. "I have one. Can I sell it to you for a ten?" she asked as she slipped the bottle of *Casillero del Diablo* into the trolley without waiting for a reply. Her man would have steak tonight, not wine. Mario looked upon Magda as his daughter. She was the only wage earner in the family; her husband was suffering from multiple sclerosis, although still at its early stages.

Magda arrived at the Studios and was greeted by the concierge, who recognised her and released the door catch to let her in. "Eleventh floor?" he asked, as he walked over to the lift and pressed the call button for her. She was greeted at her destination by Sara who held open the door for her as she manoeuvred the laden trolley. Sara squealed with delight as she unloaded platter after platter of delicacies and delights. Magda helped her arrange the dishes on the table and laid out the polystyrene plates and napkins. The wines, including the Chilean merlot, were put on top of a filing cabinet by the door to Gordon's office. Sara stood back and viewed the spread. She smiled. She had only been with this team for a month and was still eager to impress. Magda left with the bill paid and a healthy tip.

The production team wandered in and grabbed slices of pizza, quiche, chicken legs and sandwiches before they, in turn, drifted over to pour a glass of wine. Sara had opened a bottle of chardonnay and a bottle of syrah leaving the other four bottles, including the *Casillero del Diablo,* in reserve.

Gordon and Zoe were the last to arrive amid applause and more backslapping. Sara brought over a full glass of red wine for Gordon, who in a loud voice asked for quiet. "Well done, everyone, brilliant series! A toast to us all—especially to Zoe." Again, more cheers. "However," Gordon continued, lowering his voice, "Zoe will not be anchoring the next series—she has decided to go to the States, where she will be working for one of the national stations." There was silence. "I am sure you will all join me in wishing her all the best."

The team were stunned, but as one, they all responded to the toast with enthusiasm. Enquiring faces surrounded Zoe, but at the back of the office, leaning against a wall with one foot resting on it, hands behind her back, was Roz—with no expression on her face. She had been a film star in her younger days. Well, she referred to herself as a film star. True, she had made some films, but they were of the blue-tinted variety. One of the studio engineers had put together a collection of videos of Roz starring as *The Fallen Angel* onto DVD. Each new member of staff, of either gender, was given a copy, and most (including some of the females) enjoyed reliving some of the scenes in the film with the Angel herself.

Roz had moved into television when her producers felt that,

at twenty-eight, she was too old. It was a coincidence, her producer assured her, that it followed her arrest for soliciting. She enjoyed her work on *"Who the Hell Cares?"*—a consumer-oriented exposé of businesses—rising to head of research. She had even taken over for Zoe a few times when she had been indisposed.

Roz had had a difficult time over the previous twelve years with bouts of depression, aided or hindered by alcohol and drugs, but she had come through it, albeit battle-weary, which had taken a toll on her beauty. The cameras told no lies. That aside, Roz's main problem was her temper. Anger management courses had helped—she was now able to control her outbursts. Roz had dated Gordon whilst (unbeknownst to her) he was engaged to Hilary, and Roz was more than a little displeased at being dumped a week before his wedding (to which she was not invited).

Smirking inwardly, she walked over to the drinks. The unopened bottle of merlot caught her eye. "Plumy, herby, wood-oak flavour," it said on the back label. Just as she leaned forward to get the corkscrew, Gordon walked toward her. "Have you got a minute, Roz?" It was by way of an order, not a request. Holding onto the bottle and corkscrew, she followed Gordon into his office. He nodded toward the door, indicating that she should close it behind her. She chose the chair in front of his desk, where she could look over his shoulder at the panoramic view of the city through the floor-to-ceiling windows. "Great season, hey, Roz?"

She nodded.

"Roz, you know you're great, don't you?" She nodded and resisted the temptation to say that the last time he had said that was when she was laying naked under him on that couch in the corner. "I need to bring in someone young … er." He added the "er" just in time. "We need to rejuvenate the programme; some say it's getting stale."

"The ratings don't say that!" she retorted, almost spitting the words at him, her fury rising. "That job is mine—by rights, it's mine. You promised me." She stood, leaned forward, and slammed the bottle on his desk, throwing the corkscrew in his general direction. She almost tore the door from its hinges as she pulled it open and strode into the crowded office.

Everyone went quiet as she barged her way through, watching as she thumped her hands against the double-leaf doors and, ignoring the lifts, began running toward the stairs. "The Angel has flown—again," muttered one of the cameramen, recollecting his break-up with her just a few months earlier. The silence was broken by Sara asking if anyone had seen the corkscrew.

Roz galloped down two flights of stairs, her anger slowly dissipating, and by the eighth floor, she had recovered most of her composure as she walked through the door into the lobby and toward the lift. By the time it had reached the ground floor, the fire that was burning in her eyes had extinguished itself. The concierge looked up from his newspaper, recognising Roz. He was one of the few who had coveted her but whose desires had not been satiated. "Good evening, ma'am; fine show, I hear."

She looked his way in acknowledgement and took the side exit to the car park. In fact, she hardly heard his words; revenge was on her mind, revenge against them all, revenge against *her*—Zoe's replacement, whoever that would be— but especially revenge against Gordon.

The Devil's Cellar

Outwardly, Roz was calm; inwardly she was still seething as she drove to her apartment block and parked in her bay. She took the lift to the top floor, threw her keys onto the hall table, and went straight to the drinks trolley in the lounge. A large glass of vodka preceded an even larger one. She pulled the band from her long copper-tinted hair, letting it fall onto her shoulders, kicked off her shoes, and dropped her skirt. Her jumper followed the skirt onto the floor. Dressed only in her underwear, holding the vodka-filled tumbler, she wandered around the lounge, resembling a lion pacing in its cage.

Gordon left soon after Roz's outburst, going home to Hilary, their two children, and their dog. The celebrations at the studio continued for another hour. Sara stayed to clear up the remains of the food and drink, filling three black rubbish sacks. She looked around each room before turning off the lights and closing the doors. In Gordon's office, she saw the only unopened bottle of wine, the *Casillero del Diablo,* and tidily tucked it away at the bottom of the stationery cupboard beside her desk.

The first production meeting for the new series was scheduled for four weeks after the close of the last programme, giving the team a welcomed break. On the first day back, Roz arrived early and went straight into Gordon's office. She put a small box on his desk, wrapped in red foil paper with matching bow, and a un-enveloped card bearing the simple message "Sorry—love, Roz."

Part one of her plan was in place.

Sara followed her in, greeting her warmly, and went straight to the percolator to do what Gordon had told her was the most important thing of the day. She brought a mug of black coffee to Roz, who was looking out the window at the city just coming to life. She took the coffee and told Sara to distribute the files that she had collated around the board table.

Gordon arrived five minutes before the meeting was about to start, saying a general hello as he marched into his office. He saw the package on the desk, read the card, and smiled. *Whatever the peace offering is,* he thought, *for what that bitch has put me through, I deserve it!* Inside was a new mobile phone—top of the range. Sara brought in a coffee. "Ask Roz to pop in, will you please, Sara." Roz went into his office, smirking inwardly. "Thanks, sweetheart, you really shouldn't have - no need." Gordon said as he held her shoulders and kissed her on both cheeks.

"You deserve it, Gordon, for all the crap I put you through," she offered by way of an apology, trying to hide her emotions. He knew that the mobile was the latest model—but he didn't know it was also a spy phone.

"Roz, I need you to do something for me. It won't be easy, but I value your opinions, and in this case, I need the value of your judgement too."

"Oh?" She sounded intrigued.

"I need you to find me a replacement for Zoe."

She raised an eyebrow in mock surprise.

Yes, she thought to herself, *part two of my plan begins.*

The meeting was productive; there were forty possible cases to investigate with only twenty-six needed for the series. Gordon left the boardroom satisfied in the knowledge that

The Devil's Cellar

his team would come up with the best twenty-six. He asked Roz to report back to him once she had reviewed the files. As usual, she split the cases between her five researchers. She had more important things to do.

Roz went into her office, via the coffee station, and flicked the sign on the door to "Do Not Disturb." She dialled into Gordon's new mobile phone and, as predicted, found that he had set it all up and it was working to *both* their expectations. Roz turned on her computer and worked on it for the best part of two hours, constantly making notes on her pad. Satisfied, she turned the machine to stand-by, closed the notebook, and put it in the centre drawer of her desk before she locked it.

Sara's phone rang. It was her long-time boyfriend, Alan, who said, "Mum and Dad want you over for dinner on Friday. Can I come and get you?"

"Yes please," Sara said, "and come early—we can have a few moments together alone first."

Sara's mind drifted in thought. As she swivelled to and fro on her chair, she noticed the bottle of Chilean merlot in the cupboard behind her. She slipped it into her bag to take to, she hoped, her future in-laws.

Just to ensure that she would be left alone, Roz announced slightly earlier than usual, that she was going out for lunch—not that many would cherish her company if they didn't have to, unless sex was on the menu. They all got on quite well with her, but when Roz lost her temper, the resignation letters fell thick and fast on Gordon's desk. She walked into *Mario's Café* and ordered a double espresso and a tuna salad (no dressing). Greg was, as usual, sitting alone at a table by the wall, reading, with his half-eaten sandwich on the plate and a glass of cola poised on his lips.

"Hi, Greg, may I join you?" Roz said, as she sat down opposite him. He put down his drink and his magazine—*Sound and Vision Today*—and stared at her, disbelievingly, with a bemused look on his face. He, like all other new employees at the studio, had seen her greatest hits DVD. He was the latest sound engineer to join the studio and was highly regarded—young but analytically skilful. Roz considered him to be pliable too.

"Greg, I need a favour; my sound system at home isn't working right. Any chance you could pop over one evening and sort it out?"

Greg didn't need to check his diary. He was free any, and every, night. "How's tomorrow?" he asked tentatively.

Her food arrived.

"Perfect! Come over about eight and I'll make us some supper," she replied as she wrote her address on the back of a business card.

They both finished their lunches, with Greg enquiring what *exactly* the problem with the sound system was. Her responses were vague and simpering.

As they walked back to the office together, she knew that part three of her plan was under way.

The following evening, Roz was rummaging through her lingerie drawer, considering the options. She was totally confident of securing Greg's services. In the end, she decided on nothing but a pair of black fishnet hold-ups. She was sure he had never seen a naked woman, yet alone had one. She slipped on a black silk dressing gown, wrapping it around her tightly, and fastened the belt in a large bow.

At eight precisely, the intercom buzzer rang. Roz smiled and released the latch for him. As she opened the door, he thrust a bunch of garage forecourt chrysanthemums towards her. She squealed in delight, throwing her arms around his neck and kissing him forcefully on the lips. "I'm running a bit behind, Greg; go in and grab a drink while I get dressed. The beer is in the fridge." She took a step back to allow him to stare at the contours of her ample bosom and hard nipples that were pressing against the silk gown.

Roz came back into the lounge wearing a simple black skirt with a matching blouse, which she had taken great care not to button too modestly. He was staring at the sound system—not yet having been given permission to touch—with a can of lager in his hand. "Check it out, Greg, while I sort out supper," Roz said as she walked past him into the kitchen. "Can you see the problem?" she called out a few minutes later.

He had found the loose wire, which hadn't been loose thirty minutes earlier.

After the macaroni cheese and salad, followed by a fruit pie with cream, they went into the lounge to listen to a CD through the sound system that Greg had "fixed."

To the best of her knowledge, no woman had ever been committed for rape. For what she did, she could have been accused of it, but not by Greg. For forty minutes, she showed him her lifetime of experiences.

Later, they sat in opposite corners of the settee—he with a cushion over his dwindling manhood, she immodestly. "Greg, I need a favour," she said, explaining what she needed. He confirmed that it could be done and said that he would work on it over the next few days. She smiled at him, knowing that part three of her plan was nearly complete.

She pulled the cushion from him (without any resistance) and moved her head down. Her hair flowed over his loins, and his juices flowed over her tongue. Greg became a frequent visitor, in secret, as Roz had asked him. She needed to keep him enthused.

The new series was due to start broadcasting in March—four months away. Roz had short-listed three girls to interview—Elena, who was the ideal replacement for Zoe, and two others who she had found from an agency—as per part two of her plan. She had met with the two agency girls and briefed them fully on the interview techniques required and the job specification. Roz had made a call to Elena, who was doing the breakfast slot on a rival channel, and reacquainted their friendship. Although Elena was ten years younger than Roz, they had both worked together in the film industry. Elena's incursion into the business was brief and her identity, by and large, remained a secret.

Gordon conducted the interviews himself in the screen-testing suite. There were four cameras set around the room, focused on the interviewee and feeding to a split screen monitor on Gordon's desk. He could see why Roz had selected the first girl, who was beautiful, composed, and articulate. She looked good on the screen too and was definitely a prime candidate. From the office upstairs, Roz was listening, via the spy mobile, to every word. As the interview was finishing, the candidate stood and walked toward Gordon, saying, "I will do *anything* for this job."

Roz smiled and turned on the remote DVD recorder that Greg had wired for her, picking up pictures from the four cameras. The interview lasted another thirty-five minutes, mostly on the settee. Gordon left his "business card" And a promise to get in touch.

The second applicant came two days later. She was even more suitable than the first girl was and even more willing to do *anything* for the job. The recorder whirred as Gordon completed the "formalities."

On the following Monday, Elena came for her interview. In Gordon's eyes, she was ideal in every respect, and she wanted the job. Elena did *everything* to secure it. Like the previous two, her interview was captured on disc.

Gordon offered Elena the job, and after some salary negotiation, she accepted. Elena signed the contract and then showed her *enormous* appreciation to Gordon, as the DVD continued to spin.

March arrived and the team was all prepared. Elena had been made welcome and had reviewed the first four case files. Everyone was ready to record the first programme, which would be transmitted two days later. The recording went better than anyone could have expected. Elena was a natural. The first programme was punchy and amusing, and it was sure to provoke a few upsets in high places after the broadcast. Later that night, Roz and Greg returned to the studio and went into the editing suite to add Elena's "interview" to the end of the recording. Roz showed her gratitude to Greg one more time.

The previous week Roz had called a friend of hers from her past who owed her a favour. He promised to send her what she wanted, and as Roz entered the building on Friday, the concierge handed her a small but heavy box. In the privacy of her office, she unwrapped the package and put its contents, a small silver handgun, into her handbag. From her locked drawer, she took out a DVD that contained the full versions of the three interviews, which she wrapped, addressed, and took to the motorcycle couriers' office a few doors away.

Part four of her revenge plan was in place.

Roz and Gordon stayed behind in his office to watch the broadcast. The others had gone home to watch the programme with their families and to get their reactions to Elena. Gordon sat at his desk with his back to the picture windows, Roz facing him on the other side of the desk. They both turned their chairs toward the large wall-mounted plasma screen—Gordon grinning at every word, Roz grinning at the surprises yet to come.

The leather-clad courier rang the doorbell at the Gordons' residence and handed Hilary a package wrapped in brown paper.

As Elena said her farewells, the picture cut to her "interview" with Gordon. Twelve million people gasped.

Gordon jumped up with a ferocity that he had never demonstrated before, knocking over the chair in the process and sputtering, "What the fuck …?" The sentence faded as he saw Roz open her handbag, take out the gun, and point it in his direction.

The Devil's Cellar

"That job was mine. Mine, I tell you, *mine*!" she screamed as her eyes got wider and her rage mounted every millisecond.

Her temper exploded a fraction of a second before the bullet burst from the muzzle of the gun. It carved a path through Gordon's neck, piercing his carotid artery and shattering the picture window behind him into a million tiny fragments, which fell onto the pavement eleven floors below, like a sudden and violent hailstorm.

The cool air rushed in, welcoming Roz as she stepped over the dying, bloodied body and walked through the gaping window frame into the void. The Angel thought she could fly.

As she hit the ground, the devil pulled her into his cellar.

At the End of a Tether

"So, it obviously wasn't her!" Jack proclaimed at a team conference. "Unless she came back from the dead. Do we have anything else other than fingerprints to go on?"

"No sir, but I do have another really clear set," Sgt Harry Cole ventured nervously. The DI waited.

Terry Price interjected, "A guy named Frank Bowness. Nothing serious, but he has a record for disorderly conduct following a demonstration in Whitehall against the lifting of food import quotas. He's been traced to Selby in North Yorkshire, where he runs a small hardware shop."

"Contact our lot in Yorkshire and see what they know of this Frank Bowness. Then get yourself up there, if you consider it necessary."

Alan arrived early at Sara's flat, allowing them to have some private time together. They hugged and kissed lustfully, as if they hadn't seen each other for months—it had only been twenty-four hours. They had known each other for just over a year, and they were very much in love but had decided to abstain from having a full sexual relationship, both wanting to be virginal at their wedding. They hadn't yet announced their formal engagement, as Alan was waiting for his promised partnership in *Simmons and Rogers LLP, Solicitors*.

His family was staunchly Catholic, as was Sara whose parents had died of natural causes some years earlier. She missed them both, maybe her father a tad more—she was his "Twinkle." Alan and Sara had met at a church social and had found many things in common, other than their love of God and Christ. In fact, they mutually recalled that they had met when they were young children—Sara's father was a farmer and bought farm feed from Alan's father, Benjamin, a well-respected wholesaler in North Yorkshire.

Benjamin Schofield had been honoured with an OBE for his "Services to Agriculture," having done what was above and beyond the call of duty for any businessman. During the outbreak of foot and mouth disease in 2001, he had been faced with a severe financial situation because most farmers could not pay him for the merchandise that they had bought. *Schofield's Feeds Limited's* customers included over 100 out of the 130 affected farms. The devastation that the outbreak had caused to local farmers was never really fully reported, but Benjamin had said to his many loyal customers, "Don't you worry about what you owe me. You sort yourself out and settle up when you can."

He was not a rich man, but he could not face seeing his lifelong customers (and in some cases, lifelong friends too) go out of business. He went to his bank and took out a loan to cover the shortfall, using his house as security. The farmers were indebted to him, and most cleared their debts as soon as they could. In the ensuing years, his business grew, and he became what the locals termed "comfortable."

His grateful clients had recommended him for the OBE, which had been conferred on him in 2003. Benjamin was always to be seen in a suit and shirt with tie, even on the hottest of days, and he had become one of Selby's most esteemed and admired men. He was elected a Councillor and sat on the Council's Planning Committee. He was a member of the Rotary Club and vice-captain of the golf club, as well as being a supporter of the Church. Although he had been born in the latter stages of the war, his style was, deliberately, reminiscent of a gentleman of the 1930s. Despite being regarded as big in business, he was small in stature, standing barely five feet tall.

Alan and Sara arrived at seven and were greeted at the door by Eileen, Alan's mother. Sara kissed her whilst handing over the bunch of deep purple gladioli that she had carefully selected at a florist's during her lunch hour.

Eileen, unlike her ebullient husband, was demure, shy, and timid, lacking in confidence and rarely joining him at his many and varied social events. She also looked ten years older than he did. They did, however, always go to church every Sunday *en famille*. She had brought up Alan and his younger sister Janice almost single-handed; Benjamin was always too busy to help.

Sara followed Alan into the sitting room and kissed Janice tenderly. Janice, poor child, was unable to acknowledge the greeting. She had been born with cerebral palsy, leaving her profoundly disabled and requiring full-time care. Benjamin denied any responsibility for Janice's condition; it was all

The Devil's Cellar

Eileen's fault. Financially, he supported them both; morally, he gave Eileen a hard time. Physically, he made her life a misery. She cared for and loved Janice, tending to her every need day and night, sleeping in an adjoining room on the ground floor.

Benjamin had the home enlarged to accommodate the "situation," as he called it. He also had the gardens landscaped, putting in a carriage drive, with a gravel surface—he liked the sound it made as the tyres of his Mercedes crunched through the deep layers. Eileen had complained to Benjamin about the difficulty of pushing Janice's chair over the gravel. Her insolence had been rewarded with his leather belt being whipped over her shoulder, and the end slapping above her left shoulder blade—the first of many beatings. She didn't complain about the drive again and had continued to push the chair from the house to the gate and back nearly every day for twenty-three years. Eileen never complained to anybody about anything.

While the builders were working on the extension, Benjamin took the opportunity to have a wine cellar constructed in the old coal store below the house. He became passionate about his wines, using the cellar as his retreat, where his passion had become a totally absorbing infatuation. The walls had been lined with thick plaster, left rough and painted white, and the floor levelled and concreted; in the centre, the builders had formed a small drain that discharged into a gravel soakaway. The old cast iron coalhole cover remained as the only form of ventilation for the cellar, and a new, thermally insulated door had been installed at the top of the four concrete stairs that opened into what had been the old scullery and was now the extension to the kitchen.

Benjamin came into the lounge and hugged Sara as if a long-lost friend had been found. "I brought you some wine; hope you like it," she said nervously. She revered Benjamin as well as loving him as she had her father.

"Thanks, luv; I'll put it away, if I may—we're having fish tonight and a nice little chablis will be grand."

He viewed the bottle of *Casillero del Diablo* with suspicion (which he hid well) as he had become conditioned to only drink fine French wines. He would have none of this New World wine on *his* table. The meal followed the sherry, with Eileen sitting between Janice and Sara. Eileen blew on each spoonful of soup, carefully resting it on Janice's bottom lip before gently tilting it into her mouth. Some went in, some dribbled down her chin. Sara cleared the plates while Eileen busied herself with the main course: grilled plaice, new potatoes, runner beans, and a butter sauce.

Eileen cut the soft fish into small pieces for Janice and lovingly eased the food into her mouth. Eileen hardly touched her own food. Sara tried to engage Eileen in conversation; she was so excited about her new job, where she saw celebrities nearly every day. But Eileen was even more withdrawn than usual today and carried on concentrating on the task at hand. Alan and Benjamin fenced words with each other in good humour, sharing the remaining chablis and then moving on to brandies, which the ladies declined.

Eileen, the dutiful "little lady," cleared the table, kindly dismissing Sara's offer to help. When Eileen came back into the room after putting Janice to bed for the night, Alan stood in readiness to leave. His eye caught Sara's, and she stood too. "Time to go," he said, walking over to his mother and kissing her on both cheeks. Sara took Alan's lead and did likewise, also kissing Benjamin whilst giving him a light hug before they left.

"Coffee!" Benjamin barked at Eileen. She swiftly and silently stepped into the kitchen and switched on the kettle, unscrewed the coffee jar, and put a teaspoonful into a cup. He insisted on a cup and saucer—never a mug. Eileen stood staring out the window into the brightly lit garden—not looking and not seeing. The rush of steam and the click of the kettle told her that it had boiled and was ready for her to pour onto the granules. She took the coffee into the lounge and put the cup and saucer onto the small table by the side of his armchair, retreating into the kitchen once more.

"What the hell is this?" he shouted almost maniacally. Eileen dropped the cloth she was holding and ran back to the lounge. Benjamin was standing by his chair, holding the cup at arm's length toward her. As she approached, he flicked his wrist, throwing the steaming coffee over the floor in front of her; some of the liquid splashed on her torso, legs, and feet. "*Fresh* coffee, not this instant rubbish!" he screamed.

Eileen took the cup from his hand, picked up the saucer, and ran back to the kitchen, oblivious to the pain she was in. She filled a bucket with warm water and a cap full of carpet shampoo, and then scurried back to the lounge, where she fell on her knees and began to wash away the coffee stain with a brush. Benjamin strode from the room, returning just a few seconds later with his belt that hung in the lobby, ready for occasions such as this. He lashed out at her in an uncontrollable rage, with the belt flaying her bleeding back a dozen times. She neither cried out for him to stop nor tried to defend herself—she knew it only made him angrier. As he raised and lowered his belt-wielding arm, he continued his tirade of threats and warnings until he let his arm fall for the last time and walked out of the room.

Eileen paused, took a deep breath, and then continued her cleaning chores. She heard him climb the stairs and clod across his bedroom above.

With the floor looking wet but stain free, Eileen took the bucket back into the kitchen and poured the dirty water into the sink, stowing the bucket and brush in the cupboard below. She went into her room and stripped off her clothes. Her front was scarlet with burns, her back red, cut, and bloody. Taking three strong painkillers, she crawled into her bed without tending her wounds. She had become hardened to the frequent beatings and consequent pain.

The following Monday, once Benjamin left for work, she got herself and Janice fed and dressed and started out on their daily trip to the shops. It had to be daily because Eileen wasn't allowed to drive; as a result, she was unable to do a full week's shopping in one go. As she walked along the street with Janice in her wheelchair, the traders, one by one, greeted them as they passed.

"Morning, ma'am, how's the lass today?" asked Mr Hodges from the baker's.

"Not so bad, thank you, Mr Hodges. And your good lady?"

And so it went on. All the traders knew how Mr Benjamin Schofield OBE had helped their appreciative families and friends, and they were just as grateful. Eileen stopped outside the hardware store, putting the brake on Janice's chair and peeping at her lovingly before going into the shop.

The Devil's Cellar

"Morning, Mrs Schofield, how can I help you?"

Eileen told Frank, the ever-helpful shopkeeper, about her needs in detail. He finished each exchange with, "I know *exactly* what you need." And he did.

"One more thing, Frank," she asked. "Do you know a plumber who can do a small job for me and quickly?" She explained what needed to be done.

"I'm handy with me tools, Mrs Schofield, and I can find an hour or so to help you."

"Thank you, Frank; I appreciate it. Can you come over tomorrow about ten, and bring all the other bits please?"

Tuesday was Janice's day at the respite care centre; its bus came at 8.30 to collect her. The two helpers effortlessly lifted Janice onto the bus as Eileen kissed her forehead. As the bus moved away, Eileen waved even though she knew that her gesture would not be reciprocated.

Eileen took the key from the hall table drawer and unlocked the heavy cellar door. She had once been caught in there by her husband, who punished her severely for the transgression. It was his "holy of holies." She switched on the light and walked down the steps whilst surveying the room. She saw the perfect place for what she needed—behind the bookcase that contained his volumes of *The World of Wine* magazines and other specialist books.

On the adjoining table was an array of plain glasses, several corkscrews, a sommelier's tasting dish, a gold grape badge, and his apron; in excess of five hundred bottles of wine were lying in racks that reached from floor to ceiling. Under the table was a small stepladder to help him reach the bottles at the top.

At 10.05 Frank arrived, the tyres on his van scrunching as he drove to the back of the house. He unloaded the items that Eileen had bought as well as his canvas grip, which contained his tools. She showed him what she needed. He nodded and started drilling.

When he had finished, he cleared up the mess that he had made and briefed Eileen on the operation of his handiwork. He didn't quite understand exactly what it was for, but it was what she had wanted. Eileen stood by the door with her purse in her hand. "Just pay me for the materials, Mrs Schofield," he said.

She gave him two twenty-pound notes, insisting that he keep the change. She also gave him the bottle of *Casillero del Diablo* that Sara had brought, which her husband had rejected. As Frank drove away, she carried the small but heavy package that he had delivered down to the cellar. She removed the grill from the drain and poured the contents into the shallow void, followed by some water from a jug, which she poured gently on top of the powdery mix. Eileen replaced the grill and looked around one final time; she climbed the steps and locked the door behind her before returning the key to its rightful place.

All that night, Eileen sat by the side of Janice's bed, holding and stroking her hand.

Wednesday dawned. Wednesday was Benjamin's day. He allowed himself the luxury of a day off in the week, leaving strict instructions that he was not to be disturbed under any circumstances; for good measure, he left his mobile phone

The Devil's Cellar

on the dresser in his bedroom. Wednesday was the day that Benjamin played head sommelier. He donned a black satin waistcoat over his white shirt, tying a matching silk bow tie around his neck. He retrieved the key for the cellar, and without saying a word to Eileen, he unlocked the door, switched on the light, and locked the door behind him. He ceremoniously tied his apron, pinned the badge of office onto the waistcoat, and slipped the silver chain of his tasting dish around his neck. He stood back, looking admiringly at the selection of bottles, wondering where to start that day.

At 11.20, upstairs, Eileen undid the tube of epoxy resin from its bubble wrapping and squeezed the contents into the keyhole of the cellar door. Frank had said it would take twenty minutes to harden. She checked on Janice and then made herself a coffee, instant variety, and sat contemplatively on a kitchen chair, sipping from her mug.

At noon, Eileen stood up, confident that the door was well and truly locked and sealed, and kneeled down in front of the cupboard under the sink. She opened the stopcock that Frank had fitted the previous morning; on hearing the gush of water, she smiled.

Benjamin was perched on his stepladder, returning a bottle of a 2004 sauvignon blanc to its niche, when he heard the gushing of water behind him. He stepped down, assuming that the "stupid bitch" had let the sink overflow, and ran up the stairs. His key wouldn't turn, and the door wouldn't open. He looked down, seeing the water collecting on the floor, and ran back down the steps into the ever growing pool. Knowing that there was a drain somewhere, he knelt down, soaking his trousers and apron, and scrabbled around looking for the grill. He found it just by his left knee and wrenched off the cover, putting his hand into the space below in an attempt to loosen the gravel of the soakaway. All he could feel was the hardened cement that Eileen had poured in the day before. The icy-cold water was now covering his shoes as he splashed about looking for its source. In a fury, he pulled down his bookcase, with all the magazines and books falling into the pool, to reveal the open pipe in the ceiling, relentlessly spewing out the water. Benjamin's panic increased.

Even in his state, he realised who was responsible. Nevertheless, he screamed for help—but he knew no one could hear him.

As the water lapped around his knees, Benjamin planned his revenge. He smirked as he remembered the coalhole cover above him. He pulled the stepladder under the cover, but even on the top tread and on his toes, he could not reach it. The table would not budge—it had been screwed down tightly, together with the wine racks. Frantically, he pulled at the racks, dislodging the bottles that fell into the water, breaking and spilling the vintage nectar into the rising mass of water. The broken bottles sank to the floor, and with every movement Benjamin made, another piece of glass lacerated his legs. He tried rack after rack, each time more bottles falling into the deepening pool below. Eventually, one rack showed signs of movement, and with every ounce of effort, he managed to pull it away from the wall.

Eileen became flustered as she remembered the electricity. She couldn't let him be electrocuted; that would not do at all. The fuse box was in the hall cupboard, and as soon as she located the trip switch for the cellar lights, she flicked it off, plunging the cellar into darkness, save a tiny beam of

The Devil's Cellar

light that shone through the slotted keyhole in the coalhole cover.

Benjamin allowed a string of expletives to flow as he tightened his hold on the rack and dragged the unit across the floor, ripping his trousers on the broken bottles as he moved, but the cold water numbed his legs and he felt no pain from the cuts. He leaned the rack against the opposite wall so it was below the tiny beam of light and began to climb, trusting that the custom-made oak rack would take his weight, until he reached the cover. He became aware of the aroma of the wine as it filled the cellar with a heady scent. Pushing the cast iron cover open took all his remaining energy, most of which had been spent by the exertion of pulling the oak rack from the wall.

The water was lapping at his chest as he poked his head into the daylight. He yelled for help. Only two people were in earshot. One *could* do nothing; one *would* do nothing—for the moment, anyway.

Benjamin forced his left arm out alongside his head but realised that there was no chance of pulling himself through the opening. He screamed and screamed for help. Eileen turned up the volume on her radio. Benjamin had been clever when he chose the house—it was secluded and at least a mile from his nearest neighbour. The water was now overflowing from the cellar and lapping around Benjamin's neck and chin. He was freezing cold and bleeding. His screams turned into sobs.

Eileen went into the shed and carefully unwrapped the yellow fibreglass-handled pickaxe that she had bought in Frank's shop.

She walked over and stood next to Benjamin's protruding head, holding the pickaxe as if it were one of his favourite golf clubs. Despite her stealth, he heard her approach and turned his head toward her. Her back-swing seemed effortless, notwithstanding her frailty. Benjamin opened his mouth to speak, but no sound came out; he closed his eyes in disbelief as he realised what was about to happen.

His left eye was opened for him by the point of the pickaxe as she completed her swing, and the follow-through saw the point of the axe reappear from the back of his skull. His arm went limp from the elbow, his hand falling over his head and over the shaft of the weapon as if in a weak farewell wave. The water continued to flow out of the cellar, having turned a dark crimson—*just like his favourite burgundy*, thought Eileen.

The devil died in his cellar.

Eileen wiped her hands on her thighs, turned, and with a straight back and her head held high, walked toward the house as if nothing had happened. She dressed Janice in her hat and coat, and with a struggle that she had become used to, lifted her into her chair and fastened the rain cover as protection from the drizzle and wind. Eileen put on her coat tying the belt tightly around her waist. She took Benjamin's strap which was hanging on its hook, rolled it up, and tucked it in the bag that hung from the handles of Janice's chair. That strap would be used one last time.

Eileen pulled the door closed behind her, peered over the rain hood, and said to her daughter, "Let's go, sweetheart. Shall we feed the ducks?" As usual, there was no response. The drizzle eased as Eileen turned into the quiet lane and took a steady pace slightly downhill toward the village green.

The Devil's Cellar

The times that they spent by the green and the duck pond were special to her. The period of tranquillity was almost akin to her hour or so in worship each Sunday. Eileen sat on the bench that faced the church on the other side of the pond. She turned her head to the brass plate screwed to the back of the bench: "Dedicated by Benjamin Schofield OBE in loving memory of his parents Florence and Wilfred Schofield." *If only they knew*, she thought.

Eileen sat in silent contemplation for forty minutes, saying her Rosary with beads that had been a gift from her mother-in-law, and then stood. She placed her rosary beads over the back of the bench, with the crucifix dangling below the brass plate. She reached into the bag, took out Benjamin's belt, and threaded the strap though the buckle, around her wrist, and over the handle of Janice's chair, pulling it tight, binding her hand to the bar whilst at the same time saying to her daughter, "Time to go, sweetheart."

She released the brake and pushed the chair toward the church, narrowly missing the *Danger—Deep Water* sign.

The water *was* deep—and cold—and the weight of the chair pulled mother and daughter to the bottom. No one saw or heard the splash except the ducks and fish, which turned and swam away. The waters closed over the two of them. The surface calmed, and the fish and ducks returned to their business.

The devil reached for Eileen but God had the first call on her soul and took her, and Janice, to sit beside him.

The devil had to make do with the worthless soul of Benjamin, and he dragged him into *his* cellar.

As Easy as Breathing

"Dead end, was it then, Terry?" DI Harvey quipped on reading the file. "Frank Bowness isn't the villain, then?"

"No, guv, but Harry rang me when I was up there and told me that there is a set of prints from one of ours on the bottle. DS David Sumpter. Do you know him?"

Jack shook his head. "Did you speak to him?"

"No," replied Terry. "He was on leave, his dad died. Due back next Monday. Shall I go back up there?"

"No, I'll speak to someone. May save you the trip. Have a good weekend, Terry."

"You too, guv."

The news broke on Wednesday, and as soon as Frank heard it, he telephoned the police. Within the hour, DS David Sumpter arrived at the shop.

"Hello, young Dave, how are you? How are your parents?"

"Hello, Frank, we're all grand, thanks."

Frank had been the Best Man at the wedding of Dave's parents; and consequently he had known Dave since he was born. Frank always knew that he was a bright lad, even before he went to *Oxford University*. Dave attained a first class honours degree in Oriental languages and then chose a career in the police force. Frank led Dave into his flat above the shop, and as they sat in the kitchen with cups of tea, Frank recounted the events of the previous two days, not leaving out a thing. He even showed him the bottle of *Casillero del Diablo* that Eileen had given him. Dave wrote copious notes, needing few questions for clarification, as Frank was so precise in his detail.

"I feel awful, lad, I feel so responsible." Frank had his head bowed as he made the admission. "I couldn't even think about drinking that—even if I drank wine." Frank was a beer man, always had been. "Whether it's evidence or not, Dave, take it away with you, there's a good lad."

Dave stood up put his notebook away as he considered.

"No, there's no need to keep it, Frank. I'll take it from you and put it in the raffle at the charity dance next week—we are raising money for the local children's home."

The Inspector was delighted with his winnings from the raffle—a bottle of Chilean merlot.

Denise had finished her training as a beauty therapist but always had reservations about working in a salon. Her first two years after qualifying were, however, spent in a beauty parlour, and her trepidations had been realised. Although it was a well-paid job and the tips partially compensated her, she had hated every minute—she wanted to see the world. She applied to P&O for the position of masseuse, was accepted, and joined the *Oriana* at Southampton for its maiden world cruise. It was on the ship that she met and fell in love with her husband. As soon as the ship returned to England, she resigned her position, married, and moved to Yorkshire.

Twenty-five years later, with the children off her hands, Denise felt it was time to return to work. She was bored with her life and bored with her husband. He worked long hours, often leaving before she was awake and returning late at night. The weekends were his. If he wasn't required to work, he either played golf or watched football—he was a ticket holder at *Leeds United FC*—or sometimes both.

It was her husband who had come up with the idea—Denise should pick up where she had left off and return to being a beauty therapist. She had recoiled at the thought but when he added "using a mobile salon," her eyes lit up.

He had financed the mobile home for her, which was luxuriously converted and fitted out with everything a beautician would need including a massage table, a shower, a fridge, and air conditioning. Her business plan had made sense—visit the clients at their work place, allowing them to fit in treatments during their lunch hour, or at any other time that suited. The more she thought, the more obvious it became—she would provide services for men only. Business was slow to start with, and she had wondered if she had misjudged the market, but as the months passed, her fears were dispelled as she became busier and busier.

The Devil's Cellar

At forty-five, Denise still retained her figure and her beauty, but her main asset was her personality. Often her tips were nearly as much as her fee. She began to enjoy the work, always retaining the professionalism that the job demanded, wearing a white fitted tunic top and trousers with flat white shoes, and with her long blonde hair neatly tied back. She checked the appointment book and smiled when she saw that her first appointment was at *Sturridge's*, just on the edge of town. William, the finance director, was not only handsome with a good body, he was also a good tipper and sometimes he was the focus of her fantasies. Denise pulled into the car park and stopped in her usual spot. She phoned William, who said he would be there in two minutes, giving her just enough time to lower the hydraulic stabilisers and prepare the salon for its first client of the day.

After the massage, William showered and sat down in the comfortable chair as Denise brought him a freshly brewed coffee. He enjoyed the luxury of an extra ten minutes chatting with Denise while he sipped his drink. "Denise," he said, "I have recommended you to a friend; a nice chap, his name is Chein, part Chinese, as if you hadn't guessed; he will call you. I hope that's okay?"

"Delighted," she replied as he paid her the fee of £60, rounding it up to £100.

"Same time next week?" Denise asked as she made the entry in her appointment book.

William grinned and nodded. "I look forward to it more than you know."

Following her fifth, and final, job of the day, she took a few minutes for herself and sat in the rear of the vehicle, drinking a glass of cold *San Pellegrino* mineral water. She always enjoyed the extra fizziness of the water and only drank that and fresh fruit juices. She avoided alcohol and caffeinated drinks like tea, coffee, and colas. She checked her takings for the day: £465. *Not bad*, she thought, as she folded the money neatly, putting it into the wallet in her slim aluminium briefcase together with her diary. Her phone rang.

"Hello, Denise speaking," she answered brightly. "How can I help you?"

"Hi, my name is Chein—a good friend recommended me to you. Can you fit me in tomorrow?" he asked.

Denise noticed the lack of any trace of an accent. "One moment, Mr Chein, I will check my diary," she said as she lifted her briefcase onto the table and retrieved the diary. "Can-do; is tomorrow afternoon good?"

"Perfect; and by the way, Chein is my *first* name."

Denise asked for the address. She paused when he gave her the information; it was obviously a private address—she only went to businesses. "I don't usually visit clients at home," she said, "but as you are William's friend, I will make an exception." She gave him the rates; he agreed. Her diary was full for Thursday.

When Denise got home, she was not surprised to see that her husband hadn't yet returned from work. She again ate alone that night. Denise would have liked to tell someone about her day. She never told *him*—*he* didn't care.

New clients always intrigued Denise, and Chein was no

exception. His house was large and detached, bounded by high walls and electronic gates, with a beautifully landscaped front garden. She had misjudged the distance to the intercom system high on the wall, and so she called him from her mobile phone. The gates drew open, and she pulled up in front of the double garage. As she was preparing the massage couch, there was a light knock on the door. Denise turned to see her client stepping in.

"Hello, I'm Chein," he said, holding out his hand in greeting.

She hoped that her sharp intake of breath went unnoticed. Chein was over six feet tall, with long black hair and deeply tanned skin. There was little evidence of his Chinese origin. He was wearing a black towelling robe, which he dropped on the chair when Denise asked him to lay on the couch. Her training had taught her to avert her eyes in such situations, but his totally hairless body was perfection. Maybe it was the lack of pubic hair that made his manhood seem impressive. He lay face down, with elbows bent and his hands under his forehead. She began on his neck, slowly cupping and kneading his back. She noticed what she initially thought was a large mole on his cheek, just under his left eye. On a subtle, but closer check, she saw it was two tiny tattoos, seemingly Chinese characters.

Her treatment finished with a final squeeze upward from his waist. She turned away as he stood and robed. He declined a shower, but accepted a coffee after asking if he could have some brandy in it.

He sat in the chair, and they chatted for a while. He was a trader, single and wealthy. *Also pretty damn good looking*, Denise thought.

Shane Marco

"Can I make a regular booking—say every Monday and Thursday?"

Denise checked her appointment book and pencilled in the next eight slots. He paid her fee plus a £40 tip.

She got home that evening and wanted to tell *him*, but *he* wouldn't have cared.

As she arrived for her next visit, Chein was waiting at the front door in his robe; he opened the door of the van and stepped into the salon almost before she had even stopped. He slowly undid the belt from the robe, but waited until she was facing him before he took it off, again exposing his naked body to her. Her training failed her, and she stared just a fraction too long at his male components. She turned her back and busied herself, trying to regain her composure, as she told him to lay down on the couch face down. The treatment was carried out in virtual silence, but Denise was aware of how he was making her feel as she tried to shut out the thoughts from her mind. The vision of him standing there naked made her put more energy into her massage, and with each stroke, her ardour slowly began to lessen.

As she was rinsing her hands after she had finished, Chein said, almost by way of a demand as opposed to a request, "My wallet is inside, come in."

She hesitated and then stepped out of her van and walked purposefully through the front door. He led her into the kitchen and picked up his wallet from the table, paying her fee plus the usual handsome tip. He persuaded her, without too much difficulty, to have a fruit juice whilst he sipped on a strong double espresso.

Chein offered to show her around his house, and her inquisitive nature responded for her. The lounge stretched the whole width of the house with floor-to-ceiling glass doors along its length, exposing a wonderful view of the garden with its undulating lawns and flowerbeds. To the side, she could see a tennis court and a swimming pool. The dining area was on a mezzanine at the back of the lounge, with a crescent-shaped dining table with all eight chairs along one side. "So everyone can see the view as they eat," Chein explained as if reading her mind.

The tour continued upstairs, where all five bedrooms, like the ground floor, were decorated in black, red, and white. Denise used a suitably approving adjective each time she looked into a room, resisting the temptation to peek into every drawer and cupboard. He finished his tour with a visit to the pool, with its sliding roof, and then to the basement to show off his fully fitted gym.

For the rest of the day, Chein was on her mind.

On her next visit, Chein massaged Denise—externally and internally, using his hands, his lips, and all other body parts. She cancelled the rest of her appointments that day, spending her time exploring Chein as she, in turn, was explored by him.

"Darling," she started her question, "what are those tattoos on your cheek?"

"They are Cantonese symbols," he said dismissively.

"Tell me more," she said, running the tips of her fingers across his cheek.

Chein stayed silent for a moment and turned his head away from her. "My people didn't accept me as one of theirs. Too tall and looking more European than Chinese. One night I was attacked and taken to a tattooist. It says "Sei Gweino – Foreign Devil."

She wanted to tell her husband but she knew *he* wouldn't have cared.

The next time she went to Chien's, she saw a different man. There was fire in his eyes, a burning passion, she thought, as he made love to her with an energy she had never previously experienced. They showered together, and as she sat drying her hair, he left her and went downstairs. Denise put on a matching black towelling robe and went down to join Chein in the kitchen.

She gasped as she saw him from the back, slumped over the breakfast table. On hearing her gasp, he sat upright and unashamedly wiped his nose. She looked down and saw a mirror with a fine coating of white powder. Denise looked back to his face. He was smiling benignly as he held out his arms in supplication. "It's okay, baby, it's just a little coke. Makes it all so much better."

She shook her head in disbelief, slowly walking backward until she found herself against the wall. Chein walked toward her, mimicking her steps until he was pressed up to her. He kissed her roughly, and almost instantaneously any resistance that she had thought of putting up dissipated. He lifted her effortlessly onto the table and pulled open her robe. He took her roughly and without feeling, but her rising passion soon wiped out the first few distasteful moments of their lovemaking.

The Devil's Cellar

After they finished, he held her tight. "It really is okay, baby, trust me. It's like taking aspirin if you have a headache. It makes wonderful sex amazing. Try some, baby, try some."

She remained silent. All she knew was that these had been the best weeks of her life, with sexual experiences that she had never known. He led her into the lounge and lay down on the settee. Chein took a small twist of paper from his pocket and wiped the sweat from his smooth chest with his palm. He sprinkled the white powder from the packet onto the small dry patch between his nipples, beckoning Denise to him.

"Kneel down," he commanded, and pulled her head toward his chest, holding her hair tightly so that her nose was just above the mound of cocaine. He said softly, "It's as easy as breathing."

And it was. And she did. She lay still for a while, feeling the sensations permeate through her body until he pushed her head toward his groin, where she feasted on him and drank from him. Although she stayed quiet, she admitted to herself that it *was* good.

The twice-weekly regime continued, always preceded by a two-line race of nose powdering. As the weeks drew on, Denise visited Chein more frequently, but it wasn't for a mutual massage session—she wanted more cocaine. One Sunday afternoon, when Denise's husband was working, she arrived at Chein's house, without notice, to ask for some magic powder. Chein seemed preoccupied and didn't invite her in. Instead, he gave her a twist, almost throwing it at her—but his actions went unnoticed; all she was focused on were the effects of the drug.

"Wait!" he shouted, handing her a package. "Take this for me. The details are on the pack; bring me the envelope he will give you. Don't leave without the envelope." Before the last words were out of his mouth, she had closed the van door and was inhaling the snow.

Like an obedient child, she delivered the pack and received a brown sealed envelope in exchange, which she took straight back to Chein.

She knew what was in the pack and would have told her husband, but *he* wouldn't have listened.

At 8.52 on Monday, just an hour before she was due for her visit, she received a text message: "Cancel today. C."

No, no, no! she screamed to herself; *I must see him.*

Chein ignored her texts and calls, and there was no answer at his gates. Later in the afternoon, he called her. She was desperate. "I need some stuff," she pleaded.

"I can't help you," he replied disinterestedly. "I am out of the country, but if you go to that flat where you went yesterday for me, he will help."

She arrived at the apartment and was welcomed in. She told the man what she wanted, and he told her what he wanted and what his three friends wanted. She kneeled down and obliged them all in turn.

Denise became Chein's whore, dispensing sexual favours to all and sundry in return for a twist of brown paper. Sometimes he made her wait, sometimes too long, but everyone got what they wanted—eventually.

The Devil's Cellar

She should have confessed to her husband, but she knew that *he* wouldn't be bothered.

Her needs became more and more frequent, sometimes inhaling five twists a day. She ran his errands for him too, often getting a bonus in return for sex. When Chein gave her a package to take to one of his nearby friends, he promised her a snow shower on her prompt return with the envelope.

She should have confessed to her husband, but *he* wouldn't be bothered.

The short journey was anything but. An accident had caused a long delay, and she was stuck on the dual carriageway. The minutes passed; then the hours. She became agitated and anxious; she began perspiring. She gave frequent and long blasts on her horn, but to no avail. She needed a fix. She needed it *now*. The parcel was in the glove box. She knew what it contained. *Chein wouldn't be angry, would he?* she thought.

Denise drove her salon van off the road onto the verge and, without even turning off the engine, pulled the pack from its storage place, ripped off the wrapping, and ran with it to the treatment area. She opened a drawer and removed a piece of glass reserved specifically for the purpose. She sliced open the packet, tipped a bit too much cocaine onto the glass, and in greed and in need, took a large breath through her nose, inhaling it all in one attempt. She sat back on the chair for a few minutes with her eyes closed, absorbing the euphoria. She opened her eyes, saw the mess of her face in the mirror, and reached into her bag for a lipstick. As she leaned down, she felt dizzy and began to shake. She stood to get some water from the fridge. That brought no relief, and she began to get hotter and hotter and started to shake. The lipstick refused to draw a smooth line on her lips.

Before she died, she managed to write a message.

The police followed every lead, to no avail. They checked the deceased's appointment book and sat-nav. They interviewed and reinterviewed, and after investigating for three months, they were no nearer to solving the crime and were unable to follow the cocaine trail.

DS Dave Sumpter returned from leave and went in to see his Inspector. "We are stuck on the case, Dave," the Inspector said in a resigned manner. "You've a clear desk now that the Schofield case has been put to bed. Review the file, unofficially, of course, will you?" As Dave got up to leave, the inspector said, "Find them that did it, Dave; find them for her."

Dave looked through the files, reading and rereading, cross-referring, and making copious notes. He looked at the photos taken by the police at the scene. Why had she written *LIVED* on the mirror in lipstick? Why? For what reason? There *must* be a reason. He looked at the photos of the suspects, reading their profiles, their histories, their alibis, and their character testimonials. All, without exception, had impeccable references, respected in business and in pleasure. For three days, DS Dave Sumpter searched and searched for that vital clue. He knew it was there—somewhere—but where? On the fifth day, he saw it. He uploaded the file of photos onto his computer and enlarged the picture.

On the cheek of Chein Woo was a tattoo—a tattoo of Chinese characters. "*Sei Gweilo*," he said in a hushed, conspiratorial

The Devil's Cellar

tone. "*Foreign Devil!*" His three years at *Oxford University* studying oriental languages had, at last, paid rewards.

Without knocking, he went straight into the Inspector's office and slammed the two photos on his desk in front of him.

"Found him!" Dave exclaimed excitedly. "Look … the writing on the mirror … LIVED … Spell it backward; mirror it—she might have been out of her mind but …"

"DEVIL—so obvious. And where does that lead?" the Inspector responded.

"Look at Woo's face, look just there; they are Cantonese characters for *Sei Gweilo,* meaning *Foreign Devil*."

The Inspector sat back in his chair with his fingers interlocked, then stood, opened a drawer, and took out the bottle of *Casillero del Diablo* that he had won in the raffle to drink in celebration. No corkscrew and no glasses put paid to the thought. He moved the bottle to the table by the door as he said, "I'll *buy* you that glass, Dave. Come on, lad." They left the office and went to the pub where they sat and talked.   And planned.

The next morning, the Inspector went to the basement of the police station and signed into the property room as requested. He spent a few minutes looking around then signed out and left. His pocket was full, but no one noticed.

At eight o'clock on Sunday morning, as arranged, Dave got into his car, double-checked that he had with him what he had bought from the DIY store on Saturday afternoon, and drove to the Inspector's house. The Inspector was in his uniform—his right-hand jacket pocket bulging. He pulled on his gloves as he got into the car, hardly acknowledging Dave.

After a twenty-minute drive, they stopped at the gates of Chein Woo's mansion; Dave pressed the intercom button. Chein asked who it was before releasing the gate lock. They drove up and stopped at the front door. Chein was affable, welcoming them both warmly. "And how can I help you today, Inspector?"

As the words left his lips, Dave pulled a Taser stun-gun from his pocket and fired 50,000 volts into Chein. As Chein collapsed on the floor, Dave wrapped several yards of the budget-priced gaffer tape around his legs and arms. They dragged him, one hand on each arm, to the rear of the house. The door to the basement was open, and music could be heard coming from below as they unceremoniously pushed him down the short flight of stairs and sat him on the only chair in the gym. Dave was overgenerous with the gaffer tape and wound it around Chein several more times, totally immobilising him. He was screaming, protesting, enquiring, swearing—but it fell on deaf ears. The Inspector stood by a table behind Chein and took out the package from his right-hand jacket pocket together with a polythene food bag.

He used a key to tear open the pack of cocaine and poured some of its contents into the bag, which he held up to check that there was just enough powder in it. Just enough to kill him slowly.

Purposefully, he walked toward Chein and placed the bag over his head. Dave used even more tape to secure the bag and added a few holes. They didn't want him to die too quickly. They wanted to allow the inhalation of the cocaine to be prolonged. Chein's rapid breathing got deeper as the oxygen in the bag diminished; after a few minutes, it began to slow. *Too soon*, thought Dave as he cut another hole in the bag, allowing more air and more cocaine into Chein's lungs. His face was white as snow, and as the bag moved for the last time and the *Sei Gweilo* drew his last breath, the Inspector said, "May you rot in hell, you Foreign Devil."

Chein's cleaner reported the incident on Monday morning. DS Dave Sumpter was put in charge of the "Woo" case, but after four weeks, he reported to his Inspector that there were no clues, and the case should be treated as unsolved. The Inspector agreed.

On the Friday before his sixtieth birthday, some seven months after Chein Woo's death, the Inspector retired. He asked for no party and no presents. As he left his office for the last time, he picked up the bottle of *Casillero del Diablo* that had remained unopened all that time and gave it to his typist, Rachel, who cried as he kissed her farewell.

On the next Saturday morning, DS Dave Sumpter collected ex-Detective Inspector Arthur Sumpter and drove slowly to the cemetery, hardly speaking. Father and son stood by the graveside and both silently read the inscription on the headstone:

In Loving Memory Of Denise Sumpter
Wife of Arthur and Mother of David
We Cared More Than She Knew
RIP

Liver but No Bacon

"Hello, this is DS Dave Sumpter, Leeds Central. What can I do for you?"

"Thanks for calling back, Dave, my condolences." Jack wasn't in the mood for pleasantries. "We got your prints off an unopened bottle of wine that was used in a homicide down here. Bit of a long shot, I know, but can you recollect anything?"

Dave paused for a moment. "Not many bottles get past me unopened. What kind of wine was it?"

"It was a merlot, a wine called *Casillero del Diablo*. Any thoughts?"

"Funnily enough, yes. It was given to me by a local man following a particularly nasty domestic. The old man was killed with a pickaxe by the wife, who then did herself in, together with her severely handicapped daughter. I put it up as a prize in a charity dance and my dad won it."

"Any idea what happened to it?

"No," said Dave, trying to trawl his memory, "I'm pretty sure that he gave it to his secretary when he retired."

"You don't remember who she is, do you?"

"I do. She is my secretary now. Her name is Rachel Greenberg."

Rachel had rushed home and hid the bottle of *Casillero del Diablo* under her bed. Her mother, let alone her father, would not have approved. They were orthodox Jews, and wine was not allowed unless it was kosher, supervised during production by an approved rabbinical authority. As such, she was not allowed to drink this wine or even have it in the house. Rachel was not as religious as her parents were, and although she honoured and respected their religious codes at home, her approach to Judaism and its rituals was more liberal. As her father, Jacob, got older, he became more and more intolerant to life in general, and especially to how other Jews did not observe the laws of the religion. Jacob used to be a pharmacist; he had owned three shops under the name of *Green's Pharmacies* in the Moortown area of Leeds.

At sixty-six, Jacob was in a reasonable state of health, although he was always feeling sluggish and weary. After consulting with his wife, Miriam, and his accountant, Jacob had decided to sell his business. Without the pressures of work, he was able to spend more time in religious study and prayer. Every morning, he went to the synagogue to pray, which gave him the motivation to get out of bed and provided some structure to his daily routine. On Friday evening and Saturday, the Sabbath, Miriam went with him to pray. Rachel also went—sometimes. Miriam's job was to look after the house. Its cleanliness was unsurpassed, and the food was wholesome—just a bit too wholesome. Both Miriam and Jacob Greenberg were grossly overweight. Rachel wasn't. She had left school with a clutch of GCSEs, and after a year at college, where she was taught the rudiments of office routine, she settled into a secretarial job at *Leeds Central Police Station*. She loved the job and loved the variety of work that came her way. She also loved her Inspector and was upset when she learned that he was going to retire. She cried when he left.

Her brother, Ronnie, was three years older and had gone on to study A levels at school. He wasn't sure what career to follow, but he *knew* it would be either pharmacy or dentistry; he waited until the very last minute before submitting his applications for a course at University. In the end, he decided on ophthalmic optics and applied to *Birmingham University*, where he was offered a place on the condition that he achieved three A levels at grade C or above. He got all three at grade A. As Ronnie kissed his parents farewell before he left for Birmingham for the first time, he promised them that he would continue with his religious observance, and he did so for a year. At the beginning of his second year, he began to lapse. He stopped wearing his skullcap, no longer attended synagogue, and began to eat non-kosher food. But he wouldn't eat bacon.

On Thursday morning at six o'clock, Yusuf Raza had walked the short distance from his home to the mosque, just north of Leeds, to lead the congregants in prayer. Yusuf was the Imam at the mosque and needed to be there for the *Fajr* service at 6.30. He had left home without his son, Amir, who was not feeling well that morning. Amir had cystic fibrosis and was not well most mornings. Yusuf was proud of his eighteen-year-old son, but feared for his future and prayed to Allah for his good health.

When he was well, Amir led study classes to help younger members of the community understand the Holy Qur'an. His father had hoped that one day his son would follow him to become the Imam at the mosque, but he had no illusions about the life-limiting illness that needed constant medical attention. His mother, Miriah, was always there for Amir's regular, and sometimes irregular, chest physiotherapy. There were always tears in her eyes as she vigorously massaged him to help loosen the sticky mucus that congested in his lungs. He didn't see her tears as he lay face down over the edge of the bed in which he spent most of his time and which he had grown to know so well. But not as well as the Holy Qur'an, which, although he knew by heart, he read and reread at every opportunity and which he understood as well as any Muslim. His GP, Dr Khalil, was as much of a constant companion to Amir as was the Holy Qur'an; he wrote prescriptions for whichever medicine was appropriate to bring relief to Amir's discomfort and suffering.

Yusuf would always accompany Dr Khalil out the front door of the modest house, enquiring as to Amir's current condition and the results they should expect from the latest drugs. Yusuf and the doctor had walked side by side along the short path through the rusty gate, as Yusuf thanked him a dozen times. After the doctor had driven off, Yusuf had walked the few hundred yards to the local pharmacy to get the prescription dispensed. Yusuf didn't like the new owner as much as he had liked and respected Jacob Green—as he was known—and with whom he had developed a rapport just a bit stronger than the usual customer/owner relationship. Although they were of different religions, Yusuf saw Jacob as his brother. Jacob wasn't so sure, even though he was made welcome when he delivered the replacement oxygen cylinders to the Raza household. Miriah always offered Jacob refreshments, and Jacob always (politely) declined.

Yusuf had entered the mosque and had gone straight to the washroom to perform his *Wadu*—his ablutions before prayer—and to prepare himself mentally for the task ahead. The muezzin had started his call to prayer, and within five minutes there were sixty or so men ready to pray.

Following the service, and after exchanging pleasantries with the community, Yusuf had hurriedly walked home and had gone straight upstairs to see his son in order to bestow a blessing on him. Amir had been feeling a bit better, and his father had promised to bring him some breakfast and to sit and talk with him for a while. Yusuf had talked about *Jihad*. *Jihad* of the mind and spirit and the attempt to attain a harmony between faith and righteous living, the struggle to remove poverty; to fight against material and moral corruption and against social, political, and economic injustices; to restore basic human rights; to fight against tyranny and oppression; to fight against environmental pollution; and to constantly promote the advancement of human knowledge.

Amir had a different view of *Jihad*, one that he had in common with his peers and students, one that he did not share with his father. He saw *Jihad* as a real war, a war to rage on any nonbeliever, on anyone who did not follow Islam. When he taught his pupils in the mosque, Amir would talk about offensive, aggressive warfare, as exemplified by Muhammad's journey from Medina to Mecca in AD 622 and the subsequent spread of Islam. Amir was angry and

The Devil's Cellar

frustrated at his debilitating illness. Amir hated everyone who was a nonbeliever, and he ignored the duty of all Muslims to present the true teachings of Islam, which prohibits terrorism under any circumstances and forbids the killing of innocent civilians.

Amir had come downstairs to lunch, and the whole Raza family sat down to eat a meal of *Hallal* meat and salads; no pork and definitely no bacon.

Amir had grown weak, tired, and suffering badly, and Dr Khalil's visits had become more and more frequent. After his latest examination, the doctor had put away his stethoscope and closed his case without removing the prescription pad. He had smiled at Amir, shook his limp hand, and walked downstairs, followed by Yusuf. Miriah had been waiting at the foot of the stairs, wringing her hands in anguish. Dr Khalil had stayed silent for a moment before looking at them, alternately, in the eyes. He had told them that, in his opinion, Amir's condition had worsened and he now needed the constant attention and medication that could only be provided in a hospital. Miriah gasped in disbelief at what she was hearing; Yusuf held his composure. He knew that he had questions to ask but he didn't know what they were. In silence, Yusuf opened the front door and watched Dr Khalil walk to the car alone. Yusuf had turned and walked, slowly, to the back room. He had sat and prayed to Allah for his son's well-being.

The staff at the *Leeds Infirmary* took good care of Amir; there was constant nursing with regular visits from the doctors, x-rays, scans, blood tests, physical examinations, and physiotherapy all professionally administered on a regular basis.

On the evening of the fifth day following his admittance, the nurse on duty had told Yusuf and Miriah that the consultant in charge of Amir, Mr Robert Sullivan, wanted to see them at eleven o'clock the next day. At that meeting, Mr Sullivan had explained that Amir was in urgent need of surgery. Yusuf and Miriah had waited for the consultant's next words. He had told them that Amir's organs were failing and he needed a liver transplant. Soon. Very soon.

Amir had been discharged into the care of his parents and a district nurse who visited daily. Week after week, month after month went by without a call from the hospital to say that a donor had been found. Amir was unable to go to the mosque anymore. Yusuf did, and prayed. Prayed for a donor.

Ronnie had completed his second year at Birmingham University and had returned in early October to start his third, and final, year. He had spent the first few weeks travelling up and down the motorways in order to be at home for the Jewish New Year and subsequent holy days, but by the end of the month he had settled back into his routine.

He had spoken regularly with his parents on the phone and exchanged e-mails and text messages with his sister. Ronnie had become concerned at how tired his parents now looked. He had discussed it with Rachel, who had agreed with him, and although they were unable to provide any constructive solutions to the problem, they decided to have a council of war the next time Ronnie came home.

Ronnie had left Birmingham just after lunch on a Friday in mid-November to make the trip home. It was a cold, grey and wet day with the hint of wintry showers. The roads were busy, the traffic was heavy, and Ronnie had had a tiring week. The 100-mile journey should have taken no more than two and a half hours, but that day it would take nearer three. He was cutting it fine; he needed to be home before sunset, before Shabbat started. He would be late. There was no point in phoning, as his family would be on their way to the synagogue. If he had left a message, they wouldn't pick it up when they returned from prayer, as it was prohibited. He had carried on driving as fast as he could. It was touch and go whether he would be home in time.

The witnesses were unsure whose fault it had been. Some said the young lad driving the Ford; others said the driver of the car transporter. Both vehicles had been coming toward each other; both had turned right. The car had rolled twice before crashing into four oncoming vehicles and coming to rest embedded in a concrete lamppost eighty-five yards from the point of collision. The whole of the local road system had come to a halt, delaying the emergency services in getting to the accident. Ronnie had been trapped in his car, unconscious and bleeding. The gathering crowd were split between onlookers and advisors—both being experienced in their relative skills—and Ronnie had been imprisoned in his seat until the fire tender arrived to free him from the deformed car.

The traffic congestion had spread around the accident rapidly, and the worshippers leaving from both the synagogue and the mosque had heard the sirens and discussed the probable causes of the incident on their way home.

The Greenbergs had arrived home expecting Ronnie to be waiting. He wasn't. As the key turned in the lock to open the front door, the phone rang angrily. Being the Shabbat, it remained unanswered, and the caller display by the side of the phone showed a withheld number.

Rachel had been worried and ran upstairs to check, surreptitiously, her mobile phone and the house phone to see if there had been any calls from Ronnie. There hadn't been any. As she had stepped away from the phone, it screeched at her, again showing a withheld number. She didn't answer it. Composing herself, she had walked back downstairs to see her father peering through the window for a sign of his son. All he saw was a police car pulling up outside. Two officers had gotten out of the vehicle and started walking purposefully along the path to the house. Jacob's heart had sunk, and the feeling of nausea had swept over him as he moved as fast as he could to open the door, calling to his wife as he went. Rachel had followed nervously.

Although driving on the Sabbath, or even being driven, was prohibited, Jacob, Miriam, and Rachel had squeezed into the back of the police car as it drove them to Leeds Infirmary. They had been ushered into a waiting room, and despite stopping every passing nurse and man in a white coat, they could get no information as to Ronnie's condition. Miriam and Rachel had cried in each other's arms, and Jacob had sat in the corner praying, as the door opened and a young doctor came in. He had told them the bad news, adding hastily that it was too early to make any prognosis.

Eventually, they had been led through the corridors to the high dependency unit, where Ronnie was attended by two nurses. For every tube that went out of his prone body, there were two that went in. His head was bandaged, and there were large strips of plaster on his face. His eyes were black and closed, but the numerous minor cuts had dried. The monitors, which flashed and beeped steadily, went unnoticed by the Greenbergs; his mother had held Ronnie's hand with his father and sister standing behind her. Both nurses had jumped to attention as the monitor shrilled. For the briefest moment, Rachel had seen the two nurses transform into angels and then back again. One of the nurses had ushered the Greenbergs back into the waiting area as Ronnie's room filled with more nurses and doctors. It was another hour before the same young doctor had come in, looking nervous. He had told them that Ronnie was on a life support machine and that there had been no brain activity for some while. No one cried. No one spoke. No one moved. Then Rachel had howled, Miriam had cried, and Jacob had sobbed.

They had sat with Ronnie for the rest of the long night. As the first light of day filtered through the drawn blinds, a nurse had come in and ushered the family into an office. Mr Sullivan had extended his hand to each in turn, offering his sincerest regrets, before adding that they had found an organ donor card on Ronnie. He had said that the hospital needed permission from the next of kin before removing his organs. Jacob had stood up violently and told the doctor, in no uncertain terms, that they were not to remove even one hair, and under no circumstances were they to switch off the life support machines. He had sat down slowly, embarrassed and deflated by his outburst.

They had refused the offer of a taxi home, being Shabbat, and walked instead. It had been a long journey home in the cold and rain. But they didn't notice. They had hardly spoke, each locked in their own thoughts. No one ate that day; no one slept that night. Sunday had dawned and the jungle telegraph had come to life. Family, friends, congregants, neighbours had all come to comfort the family. Their rabbi had come and sat with them and talked with Jacob privately. They both knew that being an organ donor was against Jewish law. Rachel had overheard the conversation and argued that it had been Ronnie's wish to be a donor; she had asked how giving life to others could be against *any* law. The rabbi had looked down to the floor; her father had turned his back. After a few moments of silence, the three of them continued their deliberations.

Each day they had sat with Ronnie, praying for a miracle. None had come. On Wednesday morning at 9.53, Jacob had asked to see Mr Sullivan. At 10.07, Mr Sullivan had called Yusuf Raza. At 2.15, Amir had been admitted. Before he was sedated, he had heard the news that Hamid Mansur had blown up himself and nine Jews at the gates of a school in Jerusalem. Hamid had been taught by Amir, who had smiled at the news before his eyes closed as the sedative took hold.

On Thursday at eleven o'clock, Ronnie had been buried sans eyes, sans heart, sans liver, sans lungs, sans everything. The family had wept, friends had cried, and the neighbours and congregants had sobbed.

The devil had looked at Ronnie's soul and rejected it. God could have this one.

For seven days, the Greenbergs had mourned. They had sat in their house on low chairs with their clothes torn, in the custom of Jewish mourners. Jacob had recited *Kaddish*, the prayer for the departed, in the synagogue every morning and again during the prayers at his house. Visitors had come throughout the day and evening to pay their respects to the family and participate in the service. As each one came, they had left parcels of food, including sweets and chocolates, as sustenance for the mourners. On the following Thursday, after the formal period of mourning had finished, Rachel had put all the confectionery into bags to take them to the hospital as gifts for the nursing staff who had tended her brother.

She had taken the bottle of *Casillero del Diablo* too.

As she had entered the hospital, she bumped into Mr Sullivan. After enquiring about her and her parents, Mr Sullivan had relieved her of the five bags she was carrying and brought them through to his office; Rachel had explained that they were to be given to the nursing staff, adding hastily that he may, of course, help himself too.

He had asked if he could pass her family's details on to the organ recipients, as they wanted to express their gratitude. Rachel had seen no reason why he shouldn't. Once she had left, he had opened the bags and peered inside. When he had seen the label of the merlot, he had decided to set that aside for himself.

Over the ensuing months, Amir had gotten stronger and Jacob had prayed for the soul of his son. Amir would never be well, of course, but there had been no rejection of the donated liver. Mr Sullivan had been delighted with Amir's progress.

Every few weeks, the Greenbergs would get a letter, sometimes including a donation, from a grateful recipient of one of their son's organs. Jacob had passed the donations on to the families of the victims of the suicide bombing at the school in Jerusalem.

In the early summer of the following year, Amir had grown

well enough to accompany his father to the mosque. They had walked and talked; they had laughed and smiled. Both were grateful to Allah. As they had approached the mosque, Yusuf had stopped outside *Zayed's Pharmacy*. Amir had stopped too and looked enquiringly at his father. Yusuf had explained that this had been Mr Greenberg's shop and that it was Mr Greenberg's son who had given Amir his chance for life. Father and son had walked the final few yards to the mosque in silence. Amir had prayed with his father. Amir had prayed harder and longer than his father did.

On the journey home, Amir had quizzed his father about the Greenbergs. Yusuf had mentioned how Jacob had helped deliver medical supplies and had given advice, and he had said how he must have been missing his son. Yusuf had hugged Amir, and they had both cried unashamedly.

Three weeks later, Jacob was in the synagogue praying with his prayer shawl pulled over his head like a cowl. He didn't hear the door open behind him; he didn't see the beadle buzzing around and running back and forth; he didn't see the rabbi nod his approval. What he did feel was the tap on the shoulder. He turned to see Yusuf and Amir standing there in their *thobes* and *kafis*. Yusuf spoke. "May we say *Kaddish* for your son with you?" Jacob looked at the rabbi who, with a twinkle in his eyes and a slight smile on his lips, gave a cursory nod.

All three said *Kaddish* together, in perfect Hebrew, for the soul of Ronnie.

An Interview without Coffee

"Did the Greenberg girl remember what happened to the bottle?" Jack enquired.

"She did, guv, she said she gave a load of chocolates, and the wine, to the surgeon who looked after her brother. He said he would share the stuff with the nursing staff at *Leeds Infirmary*."

Mr Robert Alan Michael Sullivan FRCS was at the top of his profession. "The RAM"—the initials of his forenames—as he was called behind his back, or Rob, as he was called to his face, was tall, handsome, articulate and generally well presented. He was also an exceptionally good surgeon who was respected by his colleagues and loved by his patients. He was a master of his trade, removing and transplanting organs with an enviable success rate; he was zealous yet cautious with his disclosure of the secrets of his accomplishments. He also had a voracious sexual appetite, often bedding two or three nurses a night. He had lost his Irish brogue at about the same time that he lost the O' from his surname.

One evening, Rob was sitting alone in his apartment rolling a brandy bowl from his Waterford crystal collection in his left hand, a corona cigar with almost an inch of glowing ash hovering over a matching crystal ashtray in his right hand, and the evocative strains of Wagner's *"Ride of the Valkyries"* flowing from his *Bang and Olufsen* sound system. He had had a long day, starting at 6.00 a.m. in the operating theatre and finishing with a private consultation at 8.45 p.m. He smiled at the thought of his semi-orgy on the preceding Saturday, but at forty-two, he felt that he needed to consider retirement planning. But not tonight. Tonight he wanted to sit and relax and let the music, brandy, and cigar wash his mind. Tomorrow or the next day, he would do the thinking. What he knew was that by the time he was fifty-five, he wanted to be in the sun, on a yacht, on the French Riviera with an ever-changing lover. Or two.

His planning exercise had to wait for a further three weeks until mid-May, when he could find a slot in his work and social diaries. He packed a small bag and drove off, alone, in his convertible Bentley to his lodge in the Lake District. He rarely travelled without a companion and felt a little self-conscious at making a reservation for one at his favourite restaurant overlooking Windermere. He sat staring over the lake, sipping his coffee, imagining it being the azure-blue Mediterranean sea on a midsummer's day with the sun setting in an arc, disappearing over Spain. His thoughts were collecting, but he had always disciplined himself to ensure that he went to bed with a clear head and wrote down his ideas before retiring for the night.

Rob paid his bill, made a reservation with Enzo for the next evening, walked across the car park, and dropped into the seat of his car, lowering the roof as he lit a cigar. He was back at the lodge in less than half an hour and, still with the cigar alight, poured himself a *Jameson's Irish whiskey* and sat at his writing desk. His *Mont Blanc* pen was poised over the blank leather-bound and monogrammed notebook.

On his return home three days later, he methodically went through the list he had drawn up and made some telephone calls, lightly crossing through the names once he had set up a meeting and transferred the details to his diary. His last two calls were to his shirt-maker, *Turnball and Asser* in London's Mayfair district, and to the *Ritz Hotel,* where he reserved a room overlooking Green Park, which offered a glimpse of Buckingham Palace beyond.

Rob took a taxi to his lawyer's office, *Levy Blacks & Co.,* in the centre of town, where he met with Simon Black, the senior partner. Simon had retained the old traditions: three-piece suit, fountain pen, cigars and brandy. And freshly brewed coffee in bone china cups. Mr Black listened intently, making copious notes and asking relevant questions. Rob provided full details. Simon promised that he would consider the matters and revert to Rob within ten days.

His next meeting was at his Leeds apartment with Sayed Kahn, one of his fellow surgeons at the infirmary. Sayed had been trained in Pakistan, had served in the Pakistan Army Medical Corps, and had made no secret of the fact that he would like to return home one day. They talked over coffee, then over lunch, then over tea. Sayed realised that he would be able to go back to Pakistan sooner than he had thought.

On the ninth day after the meeting with his lawyer, Rob received the promised letter. He read and reread the five pages, pondered, mused, and deliberated. It was a hard decision but he decided to go ahead with his retirement plan.

The next appointments were with five of his favourite nurses, who he invited, individually, for a late dinner each night over a week. Over coffee, Rob explained his project; in bed (after liqueurs and brandy) they all, in turn, agreed.

After a session in the operating theatre the following week, he invited the anaesthetist, Tony, who had worked with him in the theatre that day, and with whom he had trained, into his office for a coffee and a chat. Tony liked the plan and without hesitation agreed to join Rob's team. Rob also spoke with his assistant surgeon, Matthew, who similarly liked the plan. He left the job of recruiting the remaining team members to Tony and Sayed.

Rob chose a Monday afternoon for his drive to London and manoeuvred his car through the heavy traffic to the front of the *Ritz* in Piccadilly. He passed his keys, together with a £10 note, to the porter, who effortlessly removed his case from the boot and magicked the car away to the safety of the secure car park, where it would stay for the duration of his visit to London. He took a late tea in the *Palm Court* and retired to his room on the only floor that permitted smoking, where he sat and considered the finer details of his plan whilst enjoying a cigar. The final, and several times revised, spreadsheet of his five-year business plan looked far better than he had imagined possible.

The next day, following a full breakfast, Rob walked the mile or so to his shirt-makers, where he sat, and over coffee, chose the fabrics and styles for six shirts that would be sent to his usual address within ten weeks. The very helpful Alistair took a few measurements and, without a single

The Devil's Cellar

word, updated Rob's records; then, at Rob's request, he called a taxi for him. The short journey to Cavendish Square took longer than anticipated, but Rob was in no hurry. His appointment with *Bayliss and Duncane,* Estate Agents in New Cavendish Street was not until 2.30.

Rob crossed the square and slowly walked up Harley Street, the world-famous street that enjoyed a reputation as a centre of private medical excellence. He knew that there were some 1,500 medical practitioners in and around the area, offering an extensive choice of specialists, clinics, and private hospitals. He hoped that his name would soon appear on a brass plaque on one of the doors. Rob was slightly disappointed that he saw no For Sale signs.

At 2.25, he entered the doors of *Bayliss and Duncane* and within a minute, he was ushered into Mr Duncane's office. Rob accepted the coffee offered and acquainted Mr Duncane with his requirements. Three files were presented to Rob, containing photographs, dimensions and prices. Mr Duncane must have been waiting for Rob's imperceptible, sharp intake of breath as he saw the prices. He studied the files for ten minutes, consulted the maps and his own notebook, and then pushed two of the files toward the agent, telling him that he wished to view the buildings straight away, which Mr Duncane confirmed was possible as both were empty.

Robert A. M. Sullivan FRCS selected the building in which he was going to set up the first private organ transplant service in Britain.

He took a leisurely drive back to Leeds, taking the opportunity to telephone his bank manager in order to discuss the business plan Rob had sent to him the previous week. The manager confirmed that the funding would be available subject to a personal guarantee and a first legal charge on the new property. His apartment and the lodge in the Lake District were to be sold. Rob instructed Simon Black to do whatever was necessary to ensure a rapid completion of the purchase of the four-storied building at Number 1 Harley Street, including all user licenses, title searches, and any other appropriate legalities.

Eleven months later, the *Cavendish Clinic*, as Rob had decided to call it, was in the final stages of fitting-out. Sayed had returned to Pakistan, and Rob, Tony and several other senior doctors, surgeons, anaesthetists, and technicians— not to mention nine nurses—had tendered their resignations to the director of operations at the *Leeds Infirmary*. Rob left with several presents and words of regret from his colleagues. And a list of patients needing a replacement kidney. Rob put his apartment in Leeds in the hands of agents, together with his lodge in the Lake District, and almost a year to the day since he had sat down in his lodge to formulate his plans, he was ready to move in to the lavishly furnished top floor of his clinic, which would be his new home.

The basement was set up with two operating theatres with pre-operation and recovery rooms and a pharmacy. The ground floor held the reception, kitchen and dining room, offices and consulting rooms, and the other two floors were equipped with fifteen private recovery rooms. One floor was for the recipients and one was for the donors and on each floor, there were nurses' stations and two rooms for staff in which to stay when on late or early shifts. And to be on call whenever Rob had the desire.

The removal firm, *Thos. Brown and Sons*, who came up

from London, arrived at Rob's Leeds apartment to take all of his clothes and the items he was keeping to the new flat, including his wine, spirits, cigars and crystal glasses. The furniture was being left, to be sold with the flat or disposed of by the agent. Dan, the supervisor, knocked on Rob's door at precisely nine o'clock and, together with four others, began packing all of the items that Rob pointed out to them. At 11.30, Rob closed the door of the apartment for the last time, left the keys with the porter (together with £500 as a thank you), got into his car, and set course for London. He passed the removal van just as he got onto the motorway and effortlessly accelerated away.

Dan was sitting silently in the driving seat, smiling inwardly at the booty that would *not* be delivered to Number 1 Harley Street, especially the carefully packed case hidden under a blanket in a nook in the van. *He would never know*, thought Dan. By four o'clock, the van was unloaded and the gang were on their way home with a £100 tip to share between them. And a case of assorted wines. And two shirts, still in their wrapping. But Dan wasn't going to share the wine or the shirts. He dropped off his workmates at their homes or local hostelries, as requested, before pulling up outside his semidetached house in the northern suburbs of London. He was pleased with his tally for that day, especially his shirts. The eight bottles of wine all looked promising, especially the Chilean merlot with the tempting name: *Casillero del Diablo.*

The opening party on Saturday in Rob's flat above the clinic carried over to the Sunday morning, and by arrangement, the caterers returned at midday to tidy up and take away their crockery and cutlery. By mid-afternoon the flat was back to its pristine state. Except the bed.

Sayed had flown back from Pakistan for the opening party with a list of eighteen names of young men, all of whom were willing to sell a kidney for £300. He was also holding applications from a further seventy-nine would-be donors. For each accepted donor, Sayed would receive double from the clinic for his services. Rob had a list of sixty-three would-be recipients for a kidney, all willing and able to pay, in advance, £175,000 for a healthy kidney. Plus.

Four days later, Sayed flew back to Karachi and collected three young Pakistani men from their homes. He gave them all 10,000 rupees—about £100—as agreed, which they all gave to their families before stepping into his car for the drive to the Karachi airport and the ensuing direct flight to London. None spoke English; none had ever been out of their village; none (or their families) could endure the hardships brought about by poverty for much longer. The sale of a kidney was their only hope of survival.

They would receive the balance of their money when they arrived back in Karachi after successful surgery. Sayed gave them each some sterling together with specific instructions, in both languages, as what to do on arrival in the UK. They would be met by a car and taken to the clinic. He ushered them into the departure areas and watched and waited at the door until the flight had taken off. Sayed called the clinic in London and reconfirmed the flight details and arrival time.

Rob made some telephone calls and invited three patients to attend the clinic within the next forty-eight hours for a physical examination and the promise of a kidney in return for a transfer of funds. The examination was a necessity to ensure that the risk of rejection of the donor kidneys was

The Devil's Cellar

minimal, and so a nurse took a sample of blood from each of the six would-be recipients and donors for cross-matching. The porter took the phials of blood to the laboratory a few buildings away. All tests came back clear.

Rob had set up two teams, with him heading 'A' team, together with Tony, who would work on the recipient; and Matthew heading 'B' team, dealing with the removal of the donor kidney.

At 7.00 a.m. the first donor was taken to the rear operating theatre. At 7.30, after Rob had confirmed that the money had been paid into his bank account, the first recipient was taken to the front theatre. By 11.00, both patients were back in their respective rooms, and the two medical teams met, over coffee, to discuss and analyse the morning's successful work.

The pace of work increased, with up to six operations taking place each week, but limited by the speed of recovery of the patients and the availability of recovery rooms. The success rate for the recipients was 100 percent, although regretfully, some of the donors died, but Rob did make sure that they had a dignified funeral (after removing the second kidney, of course). He also ensured that Sayed gave the donor's family an additional 10,000 rupees and a photo of the grave. Even after the cost of the funeral, Rob considered that it was good business. The *Cavendish Clinic* was grossing nearly one million pounds a week. There was no shortage of donors, and Rob considered reducing their incentive payments. Sayed objected (unbeknownst to Rob, Sayed was taking a fee from the donors). Rob also considered increasing his charges to the recipients. No one objected. He also made a regular habit of bedding two nurses every night. No one objected to that either.

The letter from the General Medical Council arrived on a Saturday and was not seen by Rob until Monday. He poured a brandy into a glass and then straight down his throat. Then another. The Council was inviting Mr RAM Sullivan, FRCS, to an "informal meeting to discuss the conduct and procedures of the *Cavendish Clinic*, its directors, and its staff."

Rob sat in his chair, lit a cigar, and reviewed in his mind the closing sentence of the final paragraph of the letter from his solicitor, Simon Black: *We strongly advise, in view of the aforementioned, that you do not proceed with this venture.*

Rob instructed his assistant to perform the operations that week. He also cancelled his night-nurses.

Rob arrived at the Euston Road headquarters of the General Medical Council at the appointed hour of noon. *High noon*, he thought. He was conducted into a large and airy but dull room, where he was greeted by three men who sat behind a heavy oak desk bearing a pile of books, notepads, a carafe of water with four glasses, and a half-full cafetière of hot coffee. Steam was rising from the three cups in front of the panel. There was no cup for him. They introduced themselves as members of the Standards and Ethics Committee and explained that this was a preliminary interview to discuss the ethics of the surgery undertaken at the *Cavendish Clinic*. They invited Rob to explain.

They listened intently to Rob's explanation of how he was saving lives and helping with poverty. They all stared at him, sipping coffee, allowing his words to flow uninterrupted.

Although there were no charges levied against him, he knew that they had made up their minds. After he explained the philosophy of the clinic for nearly an hour, they asked him to leave the room and wait in the adjoining chamber. It was less than three minutes before they called him back to tell him that disciplinary action would be taken against him by way of a formal hearing unless he resigned from the medical profession forthwith and closed down the clinic immediately.

Rob marched along the Euston Road, stamping each foot in turn on the pavement as if he were treading on the heads of the three committee members. The clinic was at the other end of Harley Street, and the half-mile journey allowed him to gather his thoughts. He walked past the reception desk, barely acknowledging the greetings proffered by Alicia, and took the waiting lift to the top floor. He turned his phones to silent, sat in his leather chair, and chain-smoked his preferred brand of cigars, trying to see a way through his predicament. He remained focused even after his fifth brandy. Rob could only see one solution.

He put on his jacket, straightened his tie, and took the lift to the basement, where his swipe-pass let him into the dispensary. Rob knew exactly what he wanted from the shelves, but nevertheless confirmed the correct dosage in the *British Pharmacopoeia*. He checked his watch with the wall clock and then pressed the buttons on the phone to connect him to reception, where he instructed Alicia to tell all the medical team to meet him, that evening, in the rear pre-operating room at seven o'clock sharp. *Sharp*, he reiterated.

At seven precisely, the eleven other members of the medical team pushed open the doors to see Rob lying on a bed with a hypodermic needle, an empty bottle of fluid, and a note by his side.

The note read, "Take all my organs; free of charge."

After a short period of reflection, the team went to work. Within thirty minutes, the body was empty. Within one hour, the chilled spares were on their way to *Leeds General Infirmary* and to the eight grateful recipients.

The devil left the soul of Robert Alan Michael Sullivan FRCS to God.

Rob's five favourite nurses all sold their story to the press. John sold his to the *Daily Mirror*; Patrick sold his to the *Daily Mail*; Alf sold his version to the *News of the World*; Raffy got good money from the BBC; Josh sold his to *BSkyB*. And wept.

ONE TURN TOO MANY

"Not the best news, I'm afraid, guv. We've got a lovely set of prints from a guy called Daevin Ramnath, but he's doing a stretch. I'll go down to Parkhurst and see if he can help. Maybe he will remember what happened to the bottle."

Dan took a semi-profile stance in front of the full-length mirror, clutching his right wrist with his left hand in the poise of a body builder. He was fit, but not that fit. He relaxed and gently brushed the imaginary creases out of his *Turnball and Asser* Oxford weave mid-blue cotton shirt. He remembered where it had come from—that bloke he brought down from Leeds to London—but he couldn't recollect where he had gotten the trousers and the navy blue knitted tie. He vaguely remembered that the gold cufflinks came from the same place as the tie, but he wasn't sure. Dan took his *Hugo Boss* navy jacket—another trophy—off the hanger in his wardrobe, and as his arm slipped through the sleeve of the jacket, he seamlessly gathered his pack of Rothman's king-size cigarettes and gold *Dunhill* lighter into his side pocket and trotted down the stairs and out of the house.

He arrived first at the *Captain's Inn* and made his way to the bar, acknowledging the greetings of several regulars, where Dermot was already pouring Dan's first pint. The barman asked him if he was waiting for his cousins, but before he could reply, Roy and Jerry came through the door and up to the bar. They were not as predictable as Dan, and the barman had to wait whilst they decided on their "first for the thirst." With a knowing look to Dermot and a returned nod, the three cousins slipped behind the bar into an empty room and sat around the small square table tucked in the corner farthest away from the door. They had business to discuss. Private business. The first three rounds and the best part of a pack of cigarettes (notwithstanding the smoking ban) were spent in chatting, catching up on the past months, and as the alcohol took hold, reminiscing about their youth.

Their mothers were sisters and had lived in the same street. Roy's and Dan's mothers were twins and younger than Jerry's mum by eighteen months. Roy's father had died soon after his son's first birthday. Jerry's dad had disappeared one summer and was never seen or heard of again. Dan's father was a mystery. No one knew who he was, not even his mother. The boys had gone to the same schools and were trouble from their first day. Within a month, the school had separated the boys by putting them in different classes. It only partially worked, and it wasn't until they were in their mid-teens that they accepted their responsibilities, and on each Friday the boys would give £20 to their mothers. Each week, that is, until they were caught. Successive periods in youth detention were followed by longer stays in prison.

The Devil's Cellar

The three sisters spent a lot of time reminiscing too. Reminiscing and regretting. Regretting the decision that they had made in coming to England from Jamaica in 1953. Maybe the boys would have been better off in Jamaica. Maybe. But they did all agree that life in England was good. Now in their late seventies, they lived together in a home for the elderly. All three of them were deteriorating, albeit at different rates, starting with the early onset of dementia. They often sat together in the bright day room of *Willow House*, not knowing each other, let alone their sons and nephews when they came to visit.

The "boys" were in their fifties and had regular jobs—Roy worked for a printing company, Jerry in a car body shop, and Dan in the removals business. But they still dabbled in a life of crime. When the opportunity arose. Today, the opportunity arose. Roy looked around furtively and leaned forward across the table inviting, by his actions, the other two to do the same. He pulled out from his pocket an envelope that held a turquoise-coloured card that read, *"The Directors and Staff of Tiffany & Co. Invites …"*

Roy excitedly explained that it was an invitation for a party to be held in early December at *Tiffany's* flagship store on Old Bond Street in London's up-market Mayfair area. This spare invitation would allow one of them to go and inspect the store. They agreed that it would be Dan, "Dapper Dan," as everyone called him because of his immaculate dress style (supplied courtesy of his customers). He had the style to blend in with the other guests although he wasn't sure that it was worth the effort and told them so. They talked for another hour, with Dan having been convinced before they left, each to go back to their homes. None of the three had partners at the moment—Jerry and Roy were divorced, whilst Dan preferred the bachelor life.

On 5 December at 7.50 p.m., Dan presented his invitation to the man in a black suit at the door of *Tiffany's,* and as he stepped over the threshold, he was presented with a glass of champagne. He smiled at the girl who held the tray, and then he wandered around the shop, with a seemingly vacant look on his face, but absorbing every aspect of the layout of the store and the contents of every cabinet and showcase. He was surprised at the prices and conceded that his reticence at the meeting with his cousins had been unfounded. Dan completed his circuit of the shop and found himself back at the entrance where he was offered another glass of bubbly. He swapped the empty glass for a full one, smiled, and expressed his thanks to the girl, who beamed a smile back at him and said, "You're welcome, sir."

Their eyes held for a moment as they appraised each other. He saw a short, overweight, and plain-looking girl in her thirties with hair that flowed long and blonde. She saw a man. She passed the tray of drinks to a colleague and began to follow Dan as he meandered around the shop, nudging his way past the other revellers. She announced that her name was Bernice and that she was the assistant store manager, formally presenting her hand for him to shake.

When Dan heard the words "assistant manager," he imperceptibly changed his attitude toward her. He smiled at her and began to gently quiz and probe her for the best part of an hour, feigning disappointment whenever she moved away to talk to others. But she quickly returned to Dan, and he greeted her each time with a broad grin.

Slowly but surely, the other guests began to leave, and

The Devil's Cellar

Bernice dismissed her colleagues one by one as the crowd thinned. Just after ten o'clock, Dan found himself alone with Bernice, who had had a few glasses too many and was a little wobbly on her feet. Dan offered to help her clear up, and without answering, she unsteadily walked over to the door and locked it from the inside, turning off most of the lights.

Dan picked up a few empty plates and enquired where the kitchen was. She led him behind a curtain to a large area, about the same size as the shop, where there was a small kitchenette, a toilet, and a door guarded by a digital lock, which he presumed was the stock room. He was interested in the stock room. Very interested. It didn't take long to clear the remnants of the party, mostly into refuse bags. As Dan was rinsing his hands, he felt her presence behind him. He forced a grin and turned around. Bernice pushed herself as close as she could to Dan with her hand casually, but purposefully, resting on his crotch. She looked up at him with pleading eyes. He thought of the reason why he was there, took a deep breath, and stooped to kiss her.

She was passionate; he was passionless. But he tried. Bernice broke away, with impish glances over her shoulder, walked toward the stock room, and moved her hand to the digital lock. Her fingers danced over the keypad, but all Dan managed to see was *5, 9, blank, blank, 8.* He cursed to himself as he responded to Bernice's beckoning and stepped into the stock room. It measured about two metres by three metres with a large table in the centre of the room covered by a black velvet cloth. Around the room were racks of jewellery in boxes, all neatly stacked and labelled. Dan's eyes moved around the room, trying to assess the quantity of jewellery there. When he had completed the visual tour, he focused on Bernice, who was lying on her back on the table with her skirt pulled up around her waist, exposing a pair of black knickers bearing a crudely drawn image of a devil cheaply printed in red on the front, ballooned by her ample belly. She beckoned him to her. After Dan did his duty, he stood up and tidied himself.

Bernice lay silently on the table with eyes wide open. He leaned over her, reached for her hands to pull her up and then discreetly turned away from her as she rearranged herself. He took the opportunity to look around the storeroom one more time. He smiled and let out an involuntary "Yes!" when he saw, written on the back of the door, the full code: *5,9,1,0,8*. Bernice misunderstood the expletive and threw her arms around Dan's waist, with her head resting between his shoulder blades.

The next day, Dan called his cousins to set up a meeting to discuss (most) of the events of the night before. The meeting was arranged for Christmas Eve at a pub near *Willow House*. They always called to see their mothers together, as it made it that much easier for them and allowed them to commiserate over a drink after the visit. They knew today would be the same sad and disconcerting visit as usual.

As Dan was getting ready to leave to see his mother and aunts, he realised that he hadn't bought anything for Christmas for his housekeeper, Matilda. She had been with him for as long as he could remember and ensured that his home was as tidy and clean as possible. She was a treasure. Dan peeled a £50 note from his money clip and presented it to her, together with a bottle of wine he randomly took from his cupboard. A bottle of *Casillero del Diablo* Chilean merlot.

The Devil's Cellar

Roy, Dan, and Jerry arrived at the home within minutes of each other, all bearing bags of gifts for their respective mothers and aunts, not forgetting the staff.

The three boys spent a long, hard hour visiting their mothers before they left and walked in silence across the road to the *Cheviot Arms,* each choking back tears of sadness. Although it was December, there was a blue sky overhead and no wind. Jerry left the other two outside lighting up cigarettes whilst he went inside to get the drinks. When he returned with a tray of three rums and three pints of lager, Dan and Roy were still sitting in the same positions as he had left them. The lagers shook them back from contemplation. The rum loosened their tongues.

The plan was set. At midnight on New Year's Eve, Jerry would drive a car onto the pavement and into the front of *Tiffany's.* There was a zebra crossing outside the shop, so there would be no kerb to mount. They decided to use a second car as a getaway, fearing serious damage to the ram-car, a lesson they had learned from a previous excursion that had cost them all five years at "Her Majesty's Country Club." Dan and Roy would go into the shop and straight through into the storeroom, while Jerry readied the other car, which he would leave parked a few yards away. Once inside the storeroom, they would put all stock from the racks onto the velvet tablecloth, grab the four corners of the cloth together, and run back to the car. Four minutes at most. After two more rounds of drinks, the three cousins walked back to their cars, hugged each other warmly, and drove off to their homes. Each would be spending their Christmas in different ways. Dan would be spending his with Bernice. He would do his duty with her as many times as necessary in order to maximise his outing on New Year's Eve.

Shane Marco

He arrived at Bernice's flat at mid-day bearing gifts—a designer-labelled watch (which he vaguely recollected as having come from a removal earlier in the year) and a box of chocolates (which he had bought from the petrol station the day before). She greeted him with a hug and offered her lips to his. She led him into her bedroom with closed curtains and dimmed lights. Bernice had a voracious sexual appetite, but Dan was a match for her in every respect. As they lay in bed, smoking their post-coital cigarettes, he carefully and purposefully asked about her life, her job, her colleagues, the shop, the stock. But mostly about the stock. He closed his eyes, concentrating on everything that she told him about the jewellery in the storeroom. Bernice talked about her life and how she had found the perfect job for her. She loved every moment—well, nearly every moment. She hated being woken in the night to attend to burglar alarm activations at the shop, which was an event that happened once every couple of months. To her frustration and annoyance, the alarm company could never find a fault. Bernice slipped out of bed at 1.30, leaving Dan to rest and regain his strength whilst she made him the best meal he had ever eaten.

She made him a steak with microwave-cooked chips for his Christmas dinner, accompanied by several cans of his favourite *Carib* beer. He refrained from drinking more than three cans, so that he could remember all the things he had learned from her. Bernice had the same.

She was not a good cook. In fact, she had never cooked for a man before. They shared dessert in bed.

At midnight, he kissed Bernice farewell and left for the safety, security, and peace of his own bed, with his head full of the layout of the shop and its contents, comforted in the knowledge that he had done more than duty had required.

Forty-five minutes before midnight on New Year's Eve, Bernice was lying in bed watching the celebrations when the phone rang. She was disappointed that it wasn't Dan who was calling her, as she hadn't heard from him for four days. She was even more disappointed when she realised that it was the control centre of the shop's burglar alarm company on the line. With a deep sigh, she acknowledged the call by confirming her password and agreed to rendezvous with the police at the shop as soon as possible. She dressed hurriedly, threw on her black cloak, walked down the two flights of stairs and pushed open the door of the block onto the street, which seemed busier than usual with cars and taxis racing to their destinations before *the* hour. Bernice didn't drive and relied on public transport for her commute to and from work. After a few minutes, a taxi pulled up across the street and a couple got out. Bernice ran across the road, excused herself, and pushed her way into the cab just as an exiting passenger was closing the door.

The police car was parked on the zigzag lines adjacent to the zebra crossing, its blue lights flashing, with PC Williams and PC Stroud standing by the front of the shop—on either side of the main door—shining their torches through the windows. Bernice introduced herself to the officers, who told her that the outside alarm had just timed itself out. She began to unlock the door, struggling as usual with the main lock at the bottom, which was connected to the alarm. Eventually, she opened the door, and the two police officers went in, with Bernice following tentatively. She went straight to the alarm panel, where the lights were flashing in seasonal colours and the siren was howling unrelentingly.

She entered her code, and the siren fell silent as the control panel returned to normality. Bernice turned on the shop's lights and went through to the stock room door to release the lock. She stood back as PC Williams pulled open the door in a dramatic manner with PC Stroud standing by his side, torch at the ready. Other than partially full shelves, the room was empty.

The officers concurred that there had been no intruder; Bernice confirmed that there had been yet another false alarm on the zone that covered the stock room. At 11.56, the police phoned their controller and then left the shop, wishing Bernice a good night and a happy New Year. As the police drove away, Bernice switched off the lights and set the alarm. She pulled the front door closed and began the ritual of locking it. She got onto her knees to put the key into the bottom lock, but it wouldn't respond to the key; she turned it to the left and to the right and then to the left again. She turned it once too many times—just as she heard the first midnight chime from Big Ben.

Jerry drove the stolen Range Rover, with its lights off, along Old Bond Street. As they heard the first chime from Big Ben over the radio, the three of them simultaneously pulled down their black woollen masks to cover their faces. The street was devoid of traffic as Jerry pushed down on the accelerator, turning hard right across the zebra crossing, over the pavement, and full throttle into the entrance of *Tiffany's*. The car reared like a horse trying to throw its rider and came to rest, having flattened the door, with its bonnet inside the shop. Roy and Dan ran inside, ignoring the screeching alarm, while Jerry went over to the Mercedes parked across the street. Dan had written the code to the stock room door on his hand, and within seconds they were inside, throwing the turquoise-coloured boxes onto the table.

The Devil's Cellar

In less than the time that they had allowed, Dan and Roy were in the Mercedes, their filled tablecloth in the boot.

PC Williams and PC Stroud were stationed in their car at the junction of Albemarle Street and Piccadilly when the call came through. With a resigned acknowledgement to the controller, they circled around and, with flashing lights and wailing siren, drove back to the shop. They reached *Tiffany's* within two minutes—a minute too late. It was PC Williams that saw the dark fluid running down the pavement. It was PC Stroud who saw the front wheel of the Range Rover resting on a hand, with its forefinger hooked through the ring of a bunch of keys.

The emergency services arrived quickly and effortlessly lifted the wrecked Range Rover off the wrecked body of Bernice Kathleen Tara O'Connell.

The devil had no use for her soul. He would wait for the three Jamaicans.

Jerry steadily drove the car back to his workshop, from where it had been borrowed. Mr Gibbs wouldn't notice the additional thirty-seven miles on the odometer of his Mercedes, just as none of the three had noticed Bernice crouching in the doorway of *Tiffany's*. Roy reversed his own car toward the boot of the Mercedes and, with Dan's help, transferred the folded cloth with hundreds of small boxes wrapped in it into the boot of his car.

They didn't notice the seven turquoise boxes that had fallen from the tablecloth. Mr Gibbs would.

The gang met at noon at Roy's flat the next day, as arranged. They had all heard the news. They sat in silence—they had never killed anyone before, never even harmed anyone either.

The pile of boxes on the floor seemed immaterial as the long, hard, and constructive discussions took place.

Mr Gibbs collected his car on 2 January and drove it home cautiously. He pulled onto his drive and walked purposefully around his repaired and repainted vehicle, nodding admiringly at the quality of restoration. He opened the bonnet Then the boot.

Mr Gibbs knew all about *Tiffany* jewellery. He had been well educated by his wife in fine jewellery and instantly recognised the boxes. He, like most of the population, had been shocked and horrified at the *"Murder at Tiffany's,"* as the press had called it. He felt a call to 999 was warranted, and within half an hour, the first of a continual stream of police arrived.

Within two hours, the police had identified the thieves and killers and had applied to the court for search warrants against the three cousins, known criminals to the police—Daevin, Jamal, and Reginald. The raids were timed for four o'clock. At three o'clock, the cousins had left their respective homes to visit their mothers for the last time on their way to the airport, where they had booked flights to Kingston, Jamaica. The receipt for the tickets was sitting in the printer tray under Roy's computer behind the pile of turquoise boxes that remained in a heap on the floor.

The arrests in the departure lounge were straightforward, and the boys put up no resistance, all giving a full confession, which the judge took into account when committing them each to an eighteen-year prison term.

The devil sat at the prison gate and waited.

SUNSET OVER BLACKFRIARS

"You got any smokes?" Dan asked DS Price. Terry had pre-empted the question and threw an opened pack of cigarettes onto the table toward Dan, who continued, "What do you want, Sergeant?"

"We are trying to locate the owner of a bottle of wine …"

Dan laughed. "Have you lot been employed by Majestic Wine Warehouse then?"

Terry waited for the laughing to stop before he continued.

"Do you remember a bottle of merlot called *Casillero del Diablo*, by any chance?"

"I usually buy a bottle of wine to forget, *not* to remember. What's so special about this wine, then?"

"It was unopened, Dan. Any thoughts?"

Dan paused as he inhaled heavily on a cigarette. "It may have been the one I gave to my cleaner, Matilda, at Christmas."

Shane Marco

"Can I take this bottle, Mum?" Debbie called over her shoulder as she opened her front door to leave for work.

Matilda took a step back from the sink so that she could see down the hallway to where Debbie was holding aloft the bottle of *Casillero del Diablo*. "Of course you can," Matilda called back. "What's the occasion?"

"Tell you later." The "Good-bye, Mum" was lost as Debbie pulled the door behind her and pushed open her umbrella to shield her from the icy rain. As she started the ten-minute walk to the station, her thoughts were focused on the end of the day, the end of the week—she hardly noticed the rain or the cold. Her mind was on other things.

Debbie smiled. It was 5.35 that Friday afternoon, the rest of the small staff at *Lerner & Co.,* Chartered Accountants had left for the weekend. Only her boss, Colin Lerner, and she remained in the suite on the first floor of a prestigious office block in New Bridge Street, along the road from Blackfriars Bridge. Colin Lerner had been waiting all day for 5.30. So had Debbie. Although he was twenty years older, she felt attracted to him like no one before. His smile made her weak at the knees; his laugh made her quiver; his eyes made her sigh. His touch made her swoon. She picked up the bottle of merlot from beside her desk and two wine glasses that she had collected earlier from the cupboard in the kitchen and walked into Colin's office, leaving the door open. "Everyone has gone," Debbie said with a glint in her eyes; she walked around his desk, putting the bottle and glasses on the small side table. Colin glanced at the bottle of wine, noticing the emblem of the devil on its neck, which reminded him of the time he had served with the Parachute

Regiment, nicknamed the Red Devils, in the Falklands conflict.

He swivelled his chair toward her, with both his elbows resting on the arms of his high-backed leather chair, his two hands touching, fingertip to fingertip. Debbie pulled her tight skirt up and straddled his thighs, leaning forward so his face nestled in her neck while she wrapped her arms around his head. His hands moved the short distance to her breasts, small, firm, and free within the soft cashmere roll-neck jumper. She had already discarded her bra and sighed deeply, her whole body tingled at his touch as he slid his hands under the waistband of her top and moved them upward. Her back arched in anticipation as she slid closer to him.

The phone rang, breaking the moment. Debbie dismounted and leaned across the desk, looking at the caller display as her fingers grasped the handset. "It's your wife." Colin noticeably slumped in his chair as Debbie answered the call.

"Good evening, Mrs Lerner, how are you?"

Helen Lerner wasn't in the mood for pleasantries and demanded to speak to her husband. Debbie put the call on hold, handed the receiver to Colin, and then discreetly left the office. "I want you home *now*!" Helen shrilled into the phone. He held the receiver at arm's length until he could hear that her ranting was running out of steam before daring to ask what the urgency was.

Colin knew better than to question Helen when she was in full flight, and he cut short the call by telling her that he would leave right away. As he did, he caught sight of Debbie standing in front of the chair in her office, with one knee resting on the seat, waving an emery board a few millimetres away from her nails, waiting. Colin stood up and opened his hands in supplication.

"It's okay," Debbie said, trying to sound light-hearted. "I'll get a cab; see you on Monday."

Colin stood transfixed for a moment; he heard the main door click as she closed it behind her.

An hour later, Colin's Jaguar pulled onto the circular drive of his house. Before he could turn off the engine, Helen opened the front door and stood on the step in hat and coat. "Just got in, dear?" Colin asked in a voice hovering between sarcasm and sympathy.

A tirade of words followed, of which he picked out a few: "listen"; "you"; "don't"; "heating"; "broken"; "cold." He glided past her and went straight through to the boiler cupboard in the utility room behind the kitchen. He caught the words "shoes"; "dirty"; "carpet" on the way. Colin opened the boiler door and pressed the reset button. After a few seconds, he heard the muffled yet comforting sound of the flames igniting and the swish of water circulating through the system. He fixed a smile on his face and walked through the kitchen, where Helen, still wearing her outerwear, was busying herself in the fridge. "All done," he said. "It will heat up soon."

Colin carried on through to the lounge, where he sank into his favourite armchair with Friday's copy of the *Times*. He stared at the back page, not seeing the words but just thinking about Debbie. Soon it would be Monday. Tonight, a quiet dinner with Helen. Tomorrow, golf in the morning

The Devil's Cellar

and a bridge session at his club in the evening, where Helen would join him for a meal. Then he would only have Sunday to get through.

On his way to golf, Colin rang Debbie's home. Matilda answered and, with a glint in her eyes, passed the receiver to her daughter. Colin apologised for the previous night and expressed his sorrow, his regrets, his frustration, and his anger. She expressed her love.

Colin got in early on Monday morning. It was January, and he was inundated with his clients' tax returns, which were all due by the end of the month. Although he had been assured by his office manager, William Prince, that they were on top of it all, he had his reservations. He looked again at the client printout and was relieved to see that there were ticks alongside most of the names and reassuring comments by the others. His diary for the day, indeed for the week, was full. Just the odd thirty-minute slot with a red cross in it. He knew what that was for. At 9.05, Debbie came into Colin's office carrying a bundle of files; she flicked on the "Do Not Disturb" sign. She placed the files on the side table and removed the untouched bottle of *Casillero del Diablo* and the two glasses, which she took back to the kitchen. Debbie returned with two mugs of steaming black coffee. She knew that Colin would provide the cream. Twenty minutes later, he did. Colin was a creative accountant and also a creative lover.

By 9.30, they had both tidied themselves up; as steadily as possible, Debbie walked back to her adjoining office and then through to the reception area, where the first client of the day was waiting.

Colin and Helen had married when they were both thirty. He had qualified as an accountant in his early twenties but chose a career in the army—a career that lasted only three years. On his discharge, he joined a small, yet profitable, practice in Essex, where he stayed for two years. A job in a large city partnership followed, and it was at that time that he formulated plans to develop his career. The vast profits that the firm was making had opened his eyes to the potential of his chosen profession.

Helen was beautiful. She had been a fashion model, working mainly in the advertising field, with the intentions of finding a wealthy husband. Colin suited her nicely, very nicely. She had no misgivings at her choice of a spouse, for it was *she* who chose *him*. Maybe her only regret was that they had no children, but the bonus was that she retained her figure. And her freedom.

When Colin he was thirty-five, he leased an office suite in the city and joined forces with Adrian, with whom he had studied and who had developed other disciplines within the accountancy profession. Adrian was a corporate man. Colin preferred the smaller clients—he found them much more interesting. And they often paid him in cash. *Lerner & Co.* expanded and after only seven years was providing a healthy income for the two partners and their families.

At their partners' meeting in early March, Adrian and Colin reviewed the year's trading. It was a cigar and champagne meeting, although neither smoked nor was there any champagne—they discussed their own accounts over coffee and biscuits. Colin was the senior partner and took 60 percent of the seven-figure profit; Adrian was entitled to only 40 percent, although his clients were responsible for contributing more than three quarters of the total billings. He wanted parity.

"It's in the agreement, Adrian," Colin reminded him. "In three years, we will both be equal partners. Only three, Adrian."

Adrian opened his mouth to speak but had second thoughts; instead, he took a sip of coffee. They reviewed their staffing levels, salaries, and bonuses. Adrian raised an eyebrow when Colin suggested the new salary and bonus for Debbie. But again, he said nothing. They discussed their various insurances, including their professional liability and their cross-indemnity life insurance coverage—the insurance that provides enough money on the death of one of them to ensure that the remaining partner has enough money to retain all of the business. They agreed that they needed to increase the sum insured on both policies. Adrian made a mental note to review the cross-indemnity policy, privately, at a later time.

The meeting finished earlier than expected, and Colin was delighted to see that Debbie was still at her desk. He looked around furtively before kissing and nibbling her neck as he whispered, "Come inside, Debs, I've got your bonus!" She got two bonuses that afternoon. And he gave her a raise.

Helen had just finished her third session of the week in the exercise room that Colin had had built at the back of the house. Her personal trainer, Ryan, made sure she had a good workout on the machines and an even better one in the bedroom afterward. Ryan liked Helen a lot. She paid well, she looked good, and she was a good lover. And she was very rich. She dreamed of going to bed with him at night and waking with him every morning. She always obeyed his instructions in the gym, and he always obeyed hers in bed. And for money, he would do anything.

Adrian sat in his office, with the life insurance policy in front of him, going over the minutes of the partners' meeting. He wasn't at all happy about the inequality of the profit share, as he wanted what was rightly his—now. He decided that he needed to do something about it.

Debbie wondered if Colin would ever be hers and hers alone. She knew that the relationship between him and his wife was fragile, and she thought long and hard about her various options. Debbie realised that it was their wealth that kept Colin and Helen together and not love. Not even affection, if what Colin told her was true—and she believed him implicitly. She decided that she needed to do something about it.

Ryan wanted Helen for himself. More accurately, he wanted Helen's money for himself. He decided that he needed to do something about it.

Following their next workout session, and their regular lovemaking session, Ryan and Helen sat opposite each other at the table in the breakfast room, both draped in white bath-sheets. Ryan's mug of steaming tea was untouched, and he was unusually silent. "What's on your mind, Ryan?" Helen asked. She wasn't sure that she wanted to hear the answer, and her body tensed.

Ryan paused for a few moments and, looking her straight in the eyes, said, "I need some money; I want to open my own gym. It's big business, and I reckon it's a money-making machine."

Helen's body relaxed as she asked what he had in mind. Ryan had thought long about it and explained to her his plans in full detail. "And just how much is this going to cost *us*?" Helen asked, emphasising the "us." Ryan feigned surprise as he inwardly smiled at her gullibility. "And how will this affect *our* time together?" she continued.

"We will always have time," Ryan said as he stood and walked behind Helen's chair, resting his hands on her shoulders before sliding them onto her breasts, pulling open the towel. As she stood, he turned her around and pushed her down onto the table. She tugged off his towel and pulled him to her, wrapping her legs around his waist. Ryan did most of the work, but he was impressed with the improvement in her inner thigh muscles.

Another 500 calories used up, she thought eight minutes later. Ryan left the house satiated and exhausted but with the promise of £250,000 from Helen. She would need, he thought, a lot more of their workout sessions to tease the one million pounds from her that he really wanted.

Adrian was the first to arrive at the office. Winter had faded, spring had arrived, and the lighter mornings had eased him out of his bed and onto a train thirty-five minutes earlier than usual. He unlocked a drawer of his desk, lifted out the partnership agreement, and stepped across to the photocopier to make a copy. Adrian stapled the pages together and put the document, together with a handwritten note, into a large envelope that he addressed for the personal attention of Gerald Reins of *Samuel, Reins and Son,* his lawyers. He left a note for his secretary asking her to send it by courier immediately and for her to tell him when it had been collected.

At 9.18, she called through to him to tell him that it had been collected, adding that the courier would telephone her once it had been delivered.

At the same time, Colin was depositing his package into Debbie, as they lay across the armchair in his office, which had become their nest over the years. After a final kiss and a mutually reassuring hug, they both got up and tidied themselves. Debbie went back to her office, and Colin sat at his desk, contemplating the cold mug of coffee. He knew that Debbie would soon bring in a replacement and he was not disappointed. She returned to her desk and pulled out a package from her bag. It was a private letter addressed to her at home, from a firm of private investigators that she had instructed to check up on Helen Lerner. The letter read, *"Following your instructions we placed surveillance on Mrs Helen Theresa Lerner for four weeks; our report is attached."* The sixty-two-page bound report made interesting reading. Very interesting reading. The thirty-seven photos were even more interesting.

William, the office manager, had noticed the bottle of merlot in the kitchen cupboard, next to the biscuits, every time he went for a tea break. As the weeks passed, the bottle was still there, untouched and gathering dust. Well, that was *his* justification for slipping the bottle into his briefcase.

Gerald Reins rang Adrian, as requested, as soon as the package landed on his desk. Adrian explained his predicament to Gerald, who promised to read the agreement and to call Adrian to discuss the issues as soon as he possibly could. Later that day, Gerald called. Adrian listened intently to what Gerald had to say; they arranged a meeting over lunch at the *Grill Bar* at the *Savoy* the following Friday. Adrian sat back in his chair, staring at the ceiling, with a smirk on his face.

Ryan arrived at Helen's for their regular workout. This time, he had a business plan in his bag; a plan that had been put together by a friend of his, and who had understood the instructions that Ryan had given to him. The folder also contained price lists from equipment suppliers and particulars from estate agents about several suitable buildings. The estimated cost of converting them had been supplied by another friend in the building trade. The total cost, allowing for contingencies, was just one million pounds. What he needed to do was to make sure that Helen did not discuss the venture with her husband.

"Let's skip the gym part today, darling," Ryan said as he stepped into the hallway, closing the door behind him and pulling Helen toward him. He hugged her tightly and kissed her hard and deep. He ran his hands up and down her back, squeezing and stroking her from her thighs to her neck before spinning her around and repeating his actions, this time on her front, pulling her tight buttocks onto his groin. She squirmed and sighed as he pulled down her shorts. He made love to her on the staircase, as he had done many times previously, before carrying her upstairs to the bedroom, where Helen repaid the deed. Several times.

Ryan needed to talk to Helen about his business plan, but he also needed to get his timing right. Generally, she had no complaint with his timing. She looked hard and long at the business plan and longer and harder at Ryan. Helen demanded to be pleasured twice more before agreeing to finance the project.

It was Colin's regimental reunion. His time in the army was unforgettable, and his tour in the Falklands, memorable. Normally he wouldn't go to the event, but this year it was different. Debbie had shown him the photographs of his wife with her personal trainer. He needed to do something about it. He sat and talked with his ex-comrades about the Falklands, about life as it was, about life as it is. After the meal, he sat at a table in the corner with Bob, who had been his best friend in the army and who would have still been in service had he not had his hand blown off by a faulty grenade. The incident injured others in the squad including Pat, who had suffered serious facial injuries.

"And how is Pat?" Colin asked.

Bob took a sip of beer before replying. "He's wild, very wild, lonely and drifting. His lust for life has turned into a lust for death. There are rumours, only rumours mind…" Bob paused momentarily and looked Colin knowingly in the eyes as he emphasised Pat's "wildness" and allowed the unsaid words to sink in. "I hear from him occasionally. As a matter of fact, we are meeting for a drink next Tuesday. Why don't you join us?"

Colin declined the offer under the pretext of another appointment but asked Bob to have Pat ring him at the office on his direct number, which he wrote on the back of a business card.

A week later, the call from Pat came. The pleasantries were brief, and Colin quickly turned the conversation to business. "For you, Col, I would do anything. You saved my life." Colin relived the moment, wondering how he had managed to deal with the horrific injuries to Bob and Pat. He knew that he had done all that he could and still regretted not

The Devil's Cellar

being able to save the other two. Pat's injuries eventually healed, but his mental scars were deeper than the one on his face.

Colin explained what he needed. Pat listened and readily agreed. He also agreed to be paid £30,000 for his services. Colin made a note of Pat's address and phone number and promised to deliver half of the fee, in cash, within the week, together with all the details that Pat would need. *Thank goodness for my cash-paying clients*, Colin thought.

Adrian called through to Colin to set a date for a meeting. Colin chose not to ask what the agenda was. He had more important things on his mind. "Wednesday or Thursday at 4.30?" Adrian suggested.

"I can do Thursday at 4.30. Can't do Wednesday, Helen is coming to the office, and we are going to dinner in town."

Adrian agreed, and as he put down the receiver, he punched the air in delight.

Helen breezed into Debbie's office at 5.15 and responded to the secretary's welcome with a cursory nod as she marched straight into her husband's office, ignoring the "Do Not Disturb" sign glowing above the door. Colin stood in greeting, smiled, and asked if her royal blue coat was a new acquisition. He heard the words "attention"; "pay"; "don't"; "birthday"; and "present." He inwardly winced as she sat in the armchair, which earlier that day had cosseted different occupants. He excused himself and walked through Debbie's adjoining office, just as she was closing the door behind her as she left for the day, and into the cloakroom.

He locked himself in a cubicle before tapping out a text

message on a new mobile phone that he had bought for the purpose. Pat, sitting behind the wheel of a stolen transit van, read the message, lit a cigarette, sent an acknowledgement, and waited.

Helen and Colin left the building in Blackfriars, just as the sun was setting. They walked side by side across the eastbound carriageway of New Bridge Street, stopping on the island refuge. Although there were gaps in the traffic, Colin held onto Helen's arm. The transit van came toward them fast, very fast, and as arranged, Pat flashed the headlights once. Colin stepped back behind Helen and, with a firm nudge in the back, pushed her into the path of the van. Had she looked up, she would have seen, behind the wheel of the transit, a man with a rugged face with a pronounced scar flowing from the middle of his forehead in a curve toward his right ear, across his cheek, and finishing at the corner of his mouth. Pat had little regard for human life and he quashed it for his own pleasure. The army had a lot to answer for. The van didn't stop or even slow down as the figure in a royal blue coat cartwheeled into the oncoming traffic. Colin, standing on the refuge, shielded his eyes and his mind and instinctively took a step backward. The driver of the articulated truck coming in the opposite direction had no time to avoid Colin, who took his last breath eight seconds after Helen took hers.

The double funeral was well attended by family, clients, staff, and friends of the couple. Adrian stood to the rear with wet eyes behind his dark glasses. He had only wanted equality, not full ownership of the practice. William stood with his head bowed in respect. Debbie sobbed bitterly. Ryan deleted Helen's numbers from his mobile phone and was soon at Chloe's house, helping *her* keep fit in the only way he knew how. He wondered when it would be the right time to tell her about his business plan.

The devil rubbed his hands in glee as he dragged two souls into the depths, where they would be spending eternity together.

Red and White

"Matilda told us that her daughter, Debbie, took the bottle. We spoke with her too, and she confirmed that she had taken the bottle of wine into her office in the city. She said that she last saw it in the cupboard in the kitchenette, but she had no idea where it went. We started talking to the staff there, but there's been a big change around since the senior partner, Mr Lerner, died. I've got the lads trying to locate the ex-staff, but it's proving to be a long job."

"Thanks, Terry, just keep me in the picture; it's been going on too long, and the trail is getting cold. We need this closed. And soon."

William Prince had been with Colin and Adrian since shortly after *Lerner & Co.* had been formed, and although he had never been promised a partnership, nor had either of the principals ever mentioned any such proposal, he had hoped that an offer would be forthcoming. The death of Colin had seemingly strengthened his position, as Adrian attempted to carry on as if nothing had happened, relying heavily on William. William's power lay in his appearance and manner, as well as his undoubted abilities. He was just over six feet tall, with an athletic build that had more to do with his genetic makeup than his fitness regime. He had a full head of wire-like, dark ginger hair, tightly curled, that ran down his face to form a tight-knotted beard. But no moustache. At work he was respected, but not liked, by the staff. Whenever one of them was called into his office, they quaked in fear. He never smiled; never joked; never socialised. Colin and Adrian had treasured him and ensured that he was well looked after. It was their weakness that was also his strength—they were soft with the staff. He was hard, but no one had ever left the firm because of William. Life without Colin would be different, and William had decided that he would broach Adrian concerning his future in the firm. But not yet. He had other matters to deal with first.

William had married Sylvia, who was also an accountant, when they were both twenty-six. He loved her smile; he loved her body; he loved her voice; he loved her hair; he loved her humour; he loved her mind. He loved her. Their wedding at *St. Bartholomew's Church* in Haslemere was attended by both families and a few of Sylvia's friends. None of William's friends came—primarily because he hadn't invited any of them— William wasn't a sociable man. The reception that followed was at the tasteful *Georgian House Hotel* along the road from the church; the couple, William Prince and his "princess," rode to the hotel in a horse-drawn carriage. That night, after they had finished making love for the first time as husband and wife, they both agreed that it had been the best, and most unforgettable, day that they had ever had, and they vowed to return to the hotel on each anniversary so as to relive the occasion.

The following morning, Sylvia and William made love; slow, uncomplicated, and unrushed love, interrupted by the untimely arrival of a waiter bringing their breakfast, which wasn't eaten until some two hours after it had been delivered.

The car came for them at noon to take them to Gatwick Airport for the start of their honeymoon, which was to be twelve days and twelve fun-filled nights at the *Ritz Carlton Hotel* situated on the Boulevard de la Croisette in Cannes on the French Riviera.

Sylvia and William arrived at the hotel just as the sun was hitting the horizon; after checking in, they left the concierge to arrange for the cases to be taken to their room by the porter. They ran down the steps from the hotel and crossed the boulevard that separated the hotel from the beach and the wine-dark sea.

Like children, they ran across the sand, ignoring the demands of a man in a yellow jacket shouting, *"Billets, monsieur, billets,"* to the edge of the ocean, where gentle waves lapped at the sand, leaving rivulets of clear water eagerly ebbing back to the sea, only to be met by the next briny in-rush. They stood silently, with Sylvia's head nestled on William's neck, and with their arms mutually hugging each other, watching as the sun sank over the horizon and disappeared from sight. The man in the yellow jacket finished tidying the deck chairs, mumbling. "Hang the expense, let's eat in the *Oyster Bar* downstairs tonight; after all, this *is* our honeymoon." William said as they finished their predinner lovemaking. Sylvia smiled and kissed his neck in approval.

After breakfast on the terrace, they left the hotel to explore the town that was notoriously famous for its chic elegance and chicer prices. Hand in hand, they walked down the right hand slope of the hotel along the boulevard toward the old town. The first designer shop oozed opulence, with just a single item being displayed in the large window: a red simulated patent leather double-breasted coat tied tightly around the mannequin's minute waist with a matching buckle-less belt. William's gasps were outdone by Sylvia's "ooohs" and "aaahs." It wasn't apparent just who dragged who into the shop, but the delight was evident on both their faces as Sylvia tried on the coat. Even before the belt was tied, William was handing over his credit card to the assistant, who was equally delighted and who had never previously made a sale within five minutes of opening. William silently grimaced when he was asked to sign the sales slip. No wonder the assistant offered to deliver the coat to the hotel, he reflected. He would grimace even more when the statement from his credit card company arrived three weeks later—he had miscalculated the exchange rate. The coat was expensive enough according to his calculation. Correctly done, the extra zero on the Barclaycard statement would take his breath away.

The coat needed matching shoes, of course, and the Rue d'Antibes, which boasted the best shopping in Europe, yielded just what she was looking for, with a promise from the sales lady to exchange them if they were not the correct shade. They proved to be perfect. William's credit card became thinner as the day progressed each time it was passed through a credit-card machine. They lunched in *Le Caveau* overlooking the old port—a simple salade de jambon with bread and a bottle of sparkling house wine.

Shane Marco

As the taxi stopped at the hotel, two porters expertly whisked the bags away, and even more expertly whisked a ten-franc note from William as they carefully deposited the bags in their room. Fatigued, William and Sylvia lay on the bed in each other's arms, and as William sang Sylvia's favourite nursery rhyme to her, they both drifted into a deep and untroubled sleep.

It was Sylvia who woke first and began the job of disentangling herself from the arms, legs, and torso of William, who indicated that he was still alive by the occasional grunt and groan. They had only been asleep for just under two hours, but Sylvia had something for her husband; something special. She smiled and began singing to herself as she leaned over the bath, turning on the taps whilst deliberating over which complimentary bath oil she should add to the water.

Sylvia knelt on the bed and kissed William to rouse him from his sleep—she would arouse him later. "Go downstairs and have a drink on the terrace, darling; you can just catch some sun. I need a bath," Sylvia whispered in his ear, adding, "Give me forty-five minutes?" as she closed and locked the bathroom door.

William sat on the terrace with a glass of wine and a bowl of olives and nuts, reflecting on the day. The accountant in him was calculating just how many francs they had spent on the first day of their honeymoon, but the warmth of the fading sun and the smoothness of the wine distracted his mind from his reckoning, and he refocused on the love he had for his wife. He finished his drink and headed back up to the room.

After closing the bedroom door behind him, he turned around to see Sylvia standing by an open wardrobe door. He

The Devil's Cellar

felt his temperature rise. And another part of his anatomy too. She was wearing her new red coat with the perfectly matching shoes. Her golden hair flowed onto her shoulders from under the red beret sitting impeccably on top of her curls. Her choice of lipstick was perfect too. William gasped as his wife and lover seductively undid the loosely knotted belt, turned slightly sideways, pushing her knee forward, and pulled the side of the coat away from her body. She was naked with the exception of the black seamed stockings and black suspender belt. He ran to her and stood at arm's length so he could inhale the sight, which would remain forever etched in his mind.

They fought over which one of them should undo his trousers, but eventually they slid down his legs onto his ankles, quickly followed by his pants. He lifted her right leg around his waist and, aided by the additional height of her red high heels, entered her smoothly. Her hip movements were in perfect synchronisation with his as they raced to a climax that came too soon for them both. Their pulsing bodies relaxed and with it their poise, as they fell back onto the bed, both chuckling uncontrollably. They lay there in a numbed state of ecstasy as they gathered their composure. He loved the way she made love; he loved the way she dressed; he loved the way she laughed; he loved the way she kissed. He adored her.

They spent their last night in Cannes in the hotel's opulent restaurant, where they ate and drank, oblivious to those around them. They reiterated the words from the vicar at their wedding ceremony as they raised their glasses to each other: "I am to my beloved," William said. "And my beloved is to me," Sylvia responded.

Life back in suburbia was good. William had the disciplines of work, as did Sylvia, who had the added responsibility of the domestic chores, which she carried out with a smile and a laugh and with a spring in her step. She pleased William in every way she could, and he reciprocated in every way he could. The red coat was always hanging on the back of the bedroom door, together with the beret and a bag containing the shoes, and it invariably featured in their lovemaking, which retained the passion, ardour, and vigour that they had enjoyed on their honeymoon. Each day they journeyed to work together and usually travelled back together in the evenings, often stopping for a drink, and sometimes supper, on their way.

When at home, William often stood in the kitchen doorway, glass of wine in hand, watching Sylvia as she busied herself cooking or preparing food; humming or singing her favourite nursery rhyme to herself with a casual smile on her lips; a smile that radiated through to her eyes; a smile that had started in her heart.

On their third wedding anniversary, which they celebrated at the *Georgian House Hotel*, Sylvia announced that she needed a change in her work life. She had decided, subject to William's approval, to retrain as a nurse. William readily agreed; he loved her and would do anything to make her happy.

Sylvia finished her training soon after their sixth anniversary and applied for, and was offered, a position at *St. Christopher's Hospice* in South London, a job that she loved and at which she proved to be extremely proficient. The satisfaction she got from the work compensated, in her eyes, for the diminution in salary. William saw just how happy she was

The Devil's Cellar

and supported her in every way possible; in order to maintain their earnings, he applied for, and got, the position as office manager at *Lerner & Co.*

As the years progressed, their careers slowly but surely began to interfere with their domestic lives. Sylvia's varied, and often long, hours meant that she and William hardly saw each other. On her night shifts, she got into bed just as he was getting up, and as he arrived home just as she was leaving for work—only a brief passing kiss on each occasion. Meals were eaten at different times; she often ate at work and he frequently ate out on his way home. The red coat gathered dust.

After a long day at the office, just a month after the tragic deaths of Colin and Helen, and as Sylvia was still at work, William decided to eat at, what had become, his favoured restaurant. The pizzeria by the station was not busy that night, and his usual place at the back was available. He contemplated the menu even though he knew what he would order—his choice was to be the lasagne. The tent-card on the table was promoting a Merlot wine from Chile; a wine called *Casillero Del Diablo.* William recollected that he had a bottle of that at home, still in the cupboard, unopened. He ordered a half bottle with his lasagne which the pretty, curvaceous, and young waitress, Gabriella, brought and carefully poured for him. As she leaned across him to put down the glass, he reached across the table for a serviette and, inadvertently, brushed his arm across her breast. She didn't recoil; she moved closer, rubbing herself on his shoulder.

William let his arm fall and moved his hand to her thigh, slowly stroking it as he moved upward under the hem of her short skirt. Gabriella moved closer, looking around to ensure they weren't being seen. His hand slid over the tops of her hold-ups onto her bare thigh. Gabriella stepped back. "Later," she said. "I finish at eleven." He ordered another half bottle of the merlot, sat back, and waited. He liked the way she looked; he liked the way she smiled; he liked the way she spoke. He lusted after her. At 10.50, they left together in a taxi to her flat. At 11.30, his lust was satiated.

William and Sylvia had not spent any meaningful time together for several months, but as she wasn't going to be working on the forthcoming weekend, they had decided to make the most of it, and both of them were looking forward to their time with each other. William had noticed that his wife had been looking a bit pale, and she had been complaining of being tired and of having headaches. Over breakfast, William suggested that she should change her schedule and work fewer hours. She shook her head violently. "No," she said, "they need me there."

"I need you more," William replied in a frustrated rising tone. He looked down at her thigh, which was exposed by her gaping dressing gown, displaying a mass of bruises.

"What the hell?" he screamed, as he pointed at her leg.

"Hazards of the job," she replied.

"Please go see the doctor, Sylvia, you don't look right."

Sylvia looked to the floor, then to her thigh, then to William.

"I will go, my love, but not this week. Maybe on my next day off."

Doctor Vickery examined Sylvia methodically. He didn't like

the bruising either. He took blood for testing and told her to call for the results the following week. When she telephoned the surgery eight days later, she was put through to Dr Vickery. "There are a few abnormalities showing on your results, Sylvia," the doctor said without any preliminaries. "I have a referral letter for you to see Johnny Smythson—good chap is Smythson." On hearing the name, Sylvia froze for a moment before mumbling a "Thank you, Doctor" and disconnecting the call. She knew Professor John Smythson. He was a respected consultant in the field of oncology.

Sylvia became a regular visitor to the hospital, where she had numerous blood tests, painful bone marrow biopsies, and lumbar punctures. After several retests, she met with John Smythson. He called her into his office and picked up her file, which he studied as if he'd just seen it for the first time. The doctor leaned forward, removed his glasses, and rested his forearms on the edge of his desk. Sylvia knew what was coming.

"Sylvia," he began, "your tests showed a few problems; there are abnormal white cells, which outnumber the red cells …"

"Doctor," she interrupted, "I am a nurse in a hospice—I understand what you are saying. Which type of leukaemia is it?"

"The worst, I am afraid," he responded, and then he paused a moment for her expected response.

"How long, Doctor?"

Sylvia waited in the kitchen for William to return from work. Although she had suspected it was leukaemia, hearing it said confirmed her worst fears. She sat at the table, a cold cup of tea untouched in front of her, holding a copy of the letter from Professor John Smythson to Dr Vickery.

She began her chemotherapy treatment at the *Mayday University Hospital*, constantly accompanied by William. He tended her, comforted her, commiserated with her; he knew that she would be all right. He loved her.

Sylvia's last days were as a patient in *St. Christopher's Hospice*, where she received the care and attention, love and kindness that she had bestowed on the patients that she had tended.

William took a taxi to the undertakers and stood nervously in the reception, waiting for Mr Blake to take him through to see Sylvia. The coffin was open and Sylvia, dressed in the red coat and beret, was lying as if asleep. "She was still as beautiful as ever," William mumbled, not noticing the excellent job Mr Blake had done, as instructed, in finding a wig that replicated her own hair, which had been lost during her chemotherapy. William's eyes welled with tears as he leaned over the coffin and kissed her forehead, slowly and longingly, one last time. He carefully unknotted the belt from her coat and slowly drew it out, wrapping it around his hand as he pulled. He stood back, fighting the tears. He failed in his struggle and cried unashamedly whilst at the same time repeatedly kissing the coiled belt on his fist. The undertaker slowly closed the lid on the casket and, with his arm around William, led him through to his office, where he again offered his sincerest condolences and a brandy. And his invoice for services rendered.

William sat alone in the car that followed the hearse to the

The Devil's Cellar

crematorium. Adrian, wearing a navy blue overcoat, was standing by the gate and bowed his head as the two cars drove through. Waiting by the chapel in two rows forming a corridor to the doors were eighteen of Sylvia's colleagues from the hospice, all in nursing uniform. Gerald, the senior doctor at the hospice, and Gladys, the head of nursing, stepped forward to greet William as he got out of the car. They both noticed the red belt around William's right fist and chose to hug him instead of the customary handshake. Silently six of the nurses stepped forward to the hearse, lifted the coffin onto their shoulders and steadily walked into the chapel between the guard of honour.

As they walked through the arch, each of the nurses gracefully placed a sunflower on the lid of the coffin. When it was resting on the bier, the music began, playing Sylvia's favourite childhood nursery rhyme, *"Frere Jacques, frere Jacques, dormez vous?"*

The devil tried to pull Sylvia into his cellar, but his grip on her red shiny coat-tail wasn't strong enough.

William woke, still sitting in his armchair, where he had fallen asleep for the fourth consecutive night following the funeral, with a nearly empty bottle of brandy by his side. The red belt was lying rolled up on the table next to the bottle. Just one bottle of alcohol remained, the bottle of *Casillero del Diablo*. But he needed spirits, not wine. He poured the remaining brandy into his glass and threw it down his throat, still hoping it would numb his mind.

Unfed, unwashed, and alone, William wandered aimlessly from room to room. Adrian had told him to take as much time away from work as he needed. William caught sight of himself in the bathroom mirror—red eyes that were still wet, furred tongue, and coated teeth shocked him into the shower. Slowly during that day, he regained composure, planning his actions systematically, starting with tidying up the house and the disposal of six empty spirit bottles.

By the end of the week, William was back to normal, as normal as he could be in the circumstances. He had put all of Sylvia's clothes in bags and phoned the hospice to ask them to collect them and deliver the contents to their charity shops.

Peter, the driver, came as arranged and loaded the bags into the van. William gave the driver an envelope to pass to head of fund-raising and the bottle of *Casillero del Diablo* for himself. Peter had known Sylvia, and as he shook William's hand in thanks, he told him that they all missed her. But not as much as William did.

Peter delivered the envelope to Joan in the fund-raising office later that day. The envelope contained a cheque for one hundred and twenty-five thousand pounds, with a note saying, "In memory of Sylvia. Please pay this into your bank promptly."

One thing was certain; the quality of designer clothes was excellent. The red belt remained in one piece despite supporting the weight of William with one end tied around his neck and the other around a rafter in the garage.

The devil missed his opportunity; William's soul went to heaven.

Evens

"There are so many sets of prints that don't match to anything," Terry Price told his boss. "We've reached a blind alley at *Lerners*; no one had any idea about the bottle. A few of the ex-employees there had gone back to their homes in India; all the others had decent alibis."

"Put some pressure on forensics, would you, Terry? I am due to retire in four years!" DI Harvey responded sarcastically.

Peter signed out from his day's shift after parking the van in the car park and, with the bottle of wine in one hand and a copy of the *Sporting Life* under his arm, got into his own car ready for his short drive home. Via the betting office. Peter liked a flutter on the dogs, or the horses, or even horseflies. Anything that moved was a fair bet for Peter. In fact, he didn't really care if it didn't move, as long as there was a wager to be had. He peered over the top of his spectacles to read the print on the label on the bottle of *Casillero del Diablo*. "Cellar of the Devil," he translated and mumbled to himself. Devil, devil … he had seen that written somewhere today. He unfolded the thumbed and penned racing paper, looking up and down the day's race cards. He started perspiring as he turned page after page until he got to the Kilbeggan meeting. There it was: Western Devil. He knew that this must be an omen; he just *knew* it—but he started to panic when he saw that the race was due to start in less than fifteen minutes.

Peter's mind moved up a gear, as did his car. He pushed down hard on the accelerator, aiming his car toward his favoured bookmakers. He calculated that the fine for parking on a yellow line outside the bookies would be worth it as long as the winning odds were greater than evens. He nearly tore the door off as he leapt out of his car without looking, and it was only the alertness of the passing motorist that avoided an unacceptable delay and a potential loss of revenue for Peter. Four minutes to go, he noted, as he scribbled his bet on the ticket: £100 to win, Western Devil, Kilbeggan, and pushed it under the glass of cash booth number three, which was the domain of Annette, together with £100. He saw the odds were 8/1—how was he going to spend the £800? As he sauntered over to the corner to watch the race on the closed circuit television, he knew that there was absolutely no possible chance of Western Devil *not* winning. He leaned back on the shelf behind him, elbows resting on its edge, his right ankle across his left, while his eyes locked on the screen as the horses came under starter's orders.

As Western Devil galloped past the winning post in first place, Peter punched the air, screaming, "Yes!" oblivious to the fact that the other four punters in the shop were tearing up their tickets. As soon as the officials confirmed the result, he sauntered over to Annette and, with a smirk on his face, presented the winning betting slip to her. "£100 in tens, please, love, the rest anyway they come." He watched her intently as she counted out the money. Her short-cut bleach-blonde hair—with matching eyebrows—was offset by her long, and obviously false, eyelashes, which encircled her violet eyes. "Just think, darlin'," he continued in his over exaggerated South London drawl, "how you and I could be spending this tonight."

"Oh, Peter, if only we could," Annette replied, flicking her eyelids rapidly in a mock flirt, "but you being married and all that …"

Peter had never seen Annette standing up; all he ever saw was her head and shoulders. And her ample bosom. Peter remembered his father's words: "When you know a woman's bra size, forget the numbers and concentrate on the letters."

It was ten years after this paternal advice, when Peter had been eighteen, before he understood what had been meant. Peter's eyes were transfixed on her breasts, which needed, he fantasised, a custom-made brassiere.

Focused as he was on her, he hardly noticed the £900 that she passed under the glass partition to him. And a slip of paper with her phone number on it.

He put £100 of his winnings in his jacket pocket for Mary. She would be pleased with him, he mused, as he folded the remaining notes and eased them into the rear pocket of his trousers. *She only needs to know what she needs to know*, he thought to himself; she would be delighted with her bonus. As he reached his car, Peter realised that he had had a double win that afternoon—not only had he earned £800 but he had also not been given a parking ticket by a warden. He put his key into the ignition lock and, before fastening his seat belt, leaned across to pick up the bottle of wine. With a broad grin on his face, he kissed the gold image of the devil printed on the shoulder of the bottle. Although he preferred beer, he considered that it may be the right time for him to change to wine—and he wondered if there was a horse called Merlot or Shiraz or …

"Halves, as usual," Peter quipped as he handed over the ten ten-pound notes to Mary. He always gave her her share in low-denomination notes, as it looked like more. She took the winnings with a disbelieving look in her eyes. She regularly found betting slips in his pockets and knew just how much he gambled, and lost, without telling her. Mary had long given up challenging him about his addiction. In fact, she relished him being out of the way as often as possible so she could spend more time with her friends.

Peter had been a scaffolder employing a dozen other labourers—a cold, dangerous, and hard occupation—and was delighted when a competitor made him an offer to buy the business from him. An offer that he couldn't (and didn't) refuse. At forty-five, Peter had calculated that he had enough money to see him and his missus through to old age. He was content. Mary wasn't. She liked her days when he was at work—she had other things to do. After four months of retirement and each other's constant companionship, they both realised that they needed some time away from each other. Mary spent more time, and money, in the gym, at the beauty parlour, at the hairdressers, and in the local shopping malls. Peter spent his time in betting offices or in front of the television and on the Internet betting sites. "You have no purpose in your life, do you?" Mary screamed at Peter during one of their regular arguments.

"You can't complain!" he retorted. And so it went on.

It was Mary's brother, Simon, who suggested to Peter that he should try doing some voluntary work, a suggestion that Peter didn't dismiss. Simon and Peter met for a drink and a chat whenever Simon was in town, and the two of them had developed a close relationship, notwithstanding their different ways of life. On Mondays, Wednesdays, and Fridays, Peter assisted at *St. Christopher's Ho*spice, doing for them whatever they needed. He liked the people there, and they liked him. He became indispensable and reliable and would often work longer hours and more days than had originally been agreed. He loved every minute of his time there. With his week split between the hospice and the betting office, Mary had her freedom back.

Mary was younger than her husband was and had kept herself in good shape. Her fortieth birthday was approaching, and Peter had been considering just what they could do to celebrate the occasion. He discussed the various options with Simon when they next met, and it was Simon who suggested a cruise to somewhere exotic. They both concurred that she would like that. Simon said that he knew a man who would get him a good deal on a *Princess Line* ship. Peter got an excellent price on a fourteen-night cruise, courtesy of his brother-in-law's contact, calling at Cannes, Florence, and Rome, as well as other interesting and romantic ports. The suite was booked on the *Grand Princess* sailing from Southampton and leaving a week before her birthday which, he calculated, would be spent in Cannes. All he had to worry about was when to tell her. He was sure she would need a new pair of shoes for the holiday.

Mary was conscious that her next birthday was a "big one."

Shane Marco

She liked being in her thirties. As did all her friends. On every other Monday, she had lunch with Joe; every Wednesday, it was with Harry; and on the occasional Friday, it was with Robert. When she could get away in the evening, she had dinner with Terry. Yes, she liked being with her friends nearly as much as they liked being with her. What they all found was that their "meals" were always calorie-negative. No food intake, but plenty of energy expended.

Simon and his twin sister Mary, who was eleven minutes older, rarely spoke. At a drunken *téte a téte* on their thirtieth birthdays, they mutually disclosed their lifestyles. Simon announced that he was gay, and Mary said that she had an insatiable sexual appetite—with the opposite sex. They agreed that the information was to be kept a closely guarded secret as the news, if it broke, would devastate their elderly—and exceedingly rich—father.

Over mugs of tea in the hospice canteen, Mike gave Peter his instructions for the day. Peter collected the keys for the red estate car and set off on his first job. He was to go to 46 Passmore Avenue to collect a patient's elderly mother, who was unable to get to the hospice in any other way to see her terminally ill daughter. As he entered the road, he was surprised to see Mary's car coming toward him, and just as he was about to flash his headlights at her in recognition, he saw her stop. Peter slowed, pulled down his sun visor, and watched in bemusement.

He knew that she was oblivious to him as she got out of the car, crossed over the road, and purposefully climbed the five steps to the front door of one of the Victorian houses that lined Passmore Avenue, just three houses away from where he was going. A tall, angular man opened the door. He was

The Devil's Cellar

in his thirties, with close-cropped hair and wearing a black T-shirt and jeans. Their lips met full on as his arm gathered her up and eased her over the threshold.

Peter felt sick. His head was pounding in confusion. His hands were tight around the steering wheel, and his knuckles were white in anger. He sat motionless for five minutes, staring at the house in disbelief.

Peter knocked on the door of Number 46, having first composed himself, and as he helped Mrs Oulten down the steps and into the car, Harry was already dining on Mary's 36C breasts. It was Wednesday.

Peter finished his day's duties feeling dejected and bewildered. He decided on his course of action, which was to be decisive and brutally harsh. But not until he had paid a visit to the betting shop. Almost absentmindedly, he selected three horses from the list, wrote out his slip, and handed his money to Annette. "I'm the one that should be unhappy, love," she said without looking up.

"Oh?" Peter said quizzically in reply.

"It's my phone that's broken," Annette said sarcastically, looking directly into Peter's eyes.

"Ah," he said as the penny dropped. "I seem to have lost your number, sorry. But how about dinner tonight?"

She scribbled her address on a scrap of paper and passed it back with the endorsed betting slip. "Steak okay? You bring the wine. 8.30?"

Peter nodded, forced a smile, and walked over to the race listings. He stared at the race cards without seeing what was written. Now he was even more confused, but he rationalised that whatever is right for the goose is also right for the gander. His three horses were unplaced in their races, and he winked at Annette as he tore up the slips and left.

Mary was already home, and the clicking that came from the bonnet of her car indicated that she hadn't been in for long. "Good day?" Peter asked as he kissed her proffered cheek.

"I had a great workout," she replied.

His voice said, "Right," in as neutral a way as he could. His brain said, *I bet you did!*

As he sorted through the post, Peter announced that he was going out with the boys that night for a pint, and as he had eaten at the hospice, he didn't need tea. Mary responded by saying that she would have a long soak in the bath and an early night.

The chocolates and flowers were courtesy of the *Tesco Metro* and the bottle of *Casillero del Diablo* wine, which was still in the boot of his car, would provide a suitable conversation piece. The address that she had given him was only about a mile from home and about the same distance from the betting office. Her flat was bright, warm, and cosy. As was Annette. She was taller and thinner than Peter had imagined her to be, with long, elegant, and shapely legs encased in black nylon.

It had been a long time since Peter had been alone with a woman in such an intimate situation, and his first kisses were nervous and hesitant. As he began to relax, his enthusiasm increased, and their kissing became longer and deeper. Her

The Devil's Cellar

lips were soft and full and fitted his perfectly; their tongues fought each other for supremacy as their hands wandered over each other's bodies. He had underestimated the size of her bust. The wine and chocolates remained unopened, the steak was left uncooked and the flowers stayed in their wrapping. The same could not be said for Annette, as she was slowly unwrapped, tenderly heated and her petals opened. They finished their meal together, both totally content and satiated with their repast.

Annette leaned across and kissed Peter's shoulder before padding off to the bathroom. As he reached down to retrieve her bra from the floor, she deftly removed his house keys from his trouser pocket. Peter smiled as he looked at the label: 36EE. She would have copies of his keys cut later and then call Peter in a wistful voice to tell him what she had found under the bed. It worked every time …

He left her bed at 10.30 and her apartment at 10.35 and within a few minutes, his car was parked on his drive. Unable to find his keys, he rang the bell and was eventually let in by a tetchy Mary, who had been woken from a deep sleep on the settee in front of the television. *Evens*, he thought. *For now.*

On Friday, he called the hospice to say he wouldn't be in but left home as usual at midmorning, parking 100 yards away from his house. An hour later, Mary's car backed out of the drive and accelerated toward the High Road, pursued at a safe distance by Peter. He knew she wouldn't see him because she never checked her rear view mirror, except for attending to her hair and makeup. She pulled into a motel car park, stopping in an available space by the fence. Peter reversed into a space on the other side, watching and waiting. A red Volvo pulled in beside Mary, and both drivers got out simultaneously and casually kissed. He was shorter and older than her "Wednesday man," with long greying hair and moustache. He wore a navy blue suit, a white shirt, and a dark tie. They walked hand in hand to the motel doors, which he held open for her, and across the reception area towards the door marked "Bedrooms this way." Robert was a gentleman. Robert always ensured that ladies came first.

On Sunday, over a midmorning brunch, Peter told Mary about her birthday present. She smiled, leaned across the table, and kissed him. "Thank you, darling," she said, "that is a wonderful present." There was a perceptible pause before she added, "But I will need some new outfits."

"Sure—you have forty-eight days to get yourself suited and booted," Peter replied helpfully.

For the rest of the day, she busied herself with lists and notes, studying maps, checking weather forecasts, reviewing the ship's layout, and memorising the itinerary.

Peter repeated his Friday ploy on Monday. This time, she drove to a modern hotel in the centre of Croydon. In the underground car park, he saw Mary embrace a casually dressed man and walk arm in arm with him to the hotel lift. Of them all, she liked Joe the best. He knew what he wanted, and she was always eager to oblige.

Annette was also eager to please, and as they sneaked more and more time together, Peter's affections for her grew. He enjoyed her company; she was uncomplicated, funny, beautiful, intelligent, and a terrific lover. She also had a 36EE bust. Peter knew that fourteen days away from her

The Devil's Cellar

would be hard. He told her so while she sobbed silently into her pillow and then more loudly in his arms.

Mary told Joe, Harry, Robert, and Terry, in turn, that she would pine for them. Each of them told her just how much she would be missed.

Mary and Peter stood side by side on the promenade deck of the *Grand Princess,* which was berthed in the docks at Southampton, each holding a glass of champagne and several rolls of paper streamers, waiting for the ship to slip her moorings and begin her journey along the Solent. Below on the quayside, a military band played Strauss's *"Radetski March,"* and a handful of port employees played the part of relatives and friends saying farewell to their loved ones. The passengers felt a tremor, the ropes were unhooked from the bollards, and the ship moved imperceptibly away from the dock. The ship's horn sounded, acting as cue for the band, who started playing *"We Are Sailing"* whilst the "relatives" waved as the shower of streamers fell over their heads and across the band.

As the days progressed, Mary and Peter began to enjoy themselves, something they hadn't done for fifteen years. Successive miscarriages had taken their toll on them both. The final straw was her fourth one, which had required a prolonged period in a psychiatric hospital. It was during that time that they made the decision not to try for a family anymore.

The days on shore were fun, and they took whichever tour was on offer; they saw the sights and experienced the atmosphere of the Mediterranean coast. The evening meals on board were wonderful, and they sat at a table with three other couples, with whom there was an instant rapport.

After dinner, they invariably went to watch a show, followed by an hour or so in the casino, where Mary became just as excited as Peter. "Stick to red or black," Peter advised as Mary sat at one of the roulette tables. "It pays evens; you will win some and lose some. When you feel you are winning—quit."

"Good morning. Breakfast," the steward called as he knocked on the door of Mary and Peter's suite. The door opened hesitantly, and he came in carrying the breakfast tray laden with food, drink, cutlery, and a bottle of champagne with two glasses. The steward chirped a "Happy birthday, madam," followed quickly with "Could you please sign, sir?" and with the faintest of bows, he slipped out of the cabin. It was 6.30 and the start of a momentous day.

The ship's tender took them ashore, where they were met by a car to take them to the heliport. Mary had always wanted to fly in a helicopter, and a flight over Cannes on her fortieth birthday seemed the appropriate little extra treat. Mary thought that the forty-five-minute flight along the coast was a magnificent birthday present, and she told Peter so. The sun was warm on their faces as they took a walk from the port to the *Palm Beach Casino* at the other end of the promenade, where they lunched and enjoyed an hour at the tables. "Remember, black or red," Peter said as he gave her €500 and she sat down opposite the croupier. "Evens indeed!" she mumbled indignantly to herself. The €360 that the croupier slid across to Mary was the result of her putting €10 on number 40. She had been betting on 40 for a while and had been just a few turns of the wheel away from losing all her money.

The taxi got them back to the port, and a tender was waiting

The Devil's Cellar

to return them, and fifty other waiting passengers, to the ship. Once on board, they went into the bar for a drink before returning to their suite to prepare for dinner. It was a formal night; dinner suits for the men, ball gowns for the ladies, and it was made even more special because the captain would be joining them at their table. They and the other couples were looking forward to sitting and talking with the handsome—and single—Captain Maynard.

Mary gasped as she opened the door to the suite. The room was adorned with flowers in vases on every conceivable flat surface, and their magnificence was enhanced by their reflections in the mirrors. The room was filled with the heady smell of roses, lilies, and that king of flowers, carnations. They had time to make love, Mary calculated after checking her watch, and she pushed Peter onto the settee, falling on top of him and plunging her lips on his. The lovemaking took longer than she had anticipated, and so she skipped her bath in favour of a shower while Peter shaved at the adjoining sink.

At eight o'clock, they were in the lobby bar for a drink; their fellow diners all toasted Mary's birthday, courtesy of *Moet en Chandon* and Peter. She had chosen a calf-length plain black sleeveless dress with a deep V-neck. The matching black jewel-encrusted choker matched her bracelet, and the delicate silver weave in her black pashmina glistened under the subtle lighting. Excitedly, the eight of them discussed their day and how much they had spent—the women meticulously describing what they had bought, the men bemoaning the cost.

As if one, at 8.25, all of the bar's occupants rose and ambled to the *Da Vinci* dining room, where an extra place had been set at their table for Captain Maynard. Other than his welcoming speech to the passengers from a distant balcony, none of the guests had spoken with him, nor indeed seen him close-up. Except Mary.

As if from nowhere, Captain Simon Maynard appeared and walked directly to Mary. He leaned down and kissed her unsuspecting cheek. "Happy birthday, Mary," he said with a huge grin on his face.

"Happy birthday to you too, Simon. How are you?" Mary replied. Almost apologetically, she introduced her twin brother to the other diners. The wine that they enjoyed that evening was from the captain's cellar and with his compliments. His company was equally enjoyable.

Mary and Peter stood shoulder to shoulder on the promenade deck, leaning on the rails and staring across the black sea toward the coastline identified only by its occasional clumps of lights flickering in the distance. They were both relaxed and easy with each other. They were alone on the deck; she was holding a glass of wine and he, along with a small cigar, a glass of beer. The waves broke against the bow of the ship, creating white radiating peaks that disappeared into the distance and causing a hypnotic sound as the ship bounced across the sea. Peter, ignoring the signs warning passengers not to, flicked his cigar towards the water, took the glass from Mary's hand and placed it, together with his, on the deck.

He bent down, looked around furtively, moved his hands onto Mary's calves and slowly downward to her ankles. With the unforgotten skills of an ex-scaffolder hoisting three scaffold boards, Peter effortlessly lifted Mary and tossed her over the railing. Her mouth opened as if to scream, but before any sound came out, it was filled with salty, cold, and fatal seawater. Her pashmina, having been caught on a jutting bolt, flapped in the breeze and was the only evidence of Mary that remained. Without hesitation, Peter picked up the two glasses from the deck and walked toward the door to one of the ship's lounges. He looked over his shoulder and, speaking to the fluttering shawl, said, "Another glass of wine, darling?"

Neptune pulled Mary's body to the bottom before releasing her soul to the grateful arms of the devil.

Evens, Peter mumbled to himself.

Unintended Consequences

"Get in here, Terry! You can tell me face to face, not on the phone," Jack barked down the handset. The superintendent was putting pressure on DI Harvey for a conclusion to the murder. Jack, in turn, was putting pressure on his sergeant, who was doing the same to his detective-constables.

"Guv, sorry about that. I was waiting for a call from a mate. He knows Annette Smith; her prints were on the bottle. Her *left* hand prints."

"Okay, Terry, get on with it. I'm getting hassled by the super."

Captain Maynard closed his log. "Missing, presumed drowned," he wrote, then proceeded to complete all the necessary forms and reports needed by the authorities—including the life insurance company. He considered phoning his father but decided that, in order to lessen the shock, he needed to tell him face to face. And to ensure that the will was suitably, and promptly, changed. He smiled at the thought of the inheritance and whether the news of his daughter's death would hasten that of his father's. Peter knew he would have to wait for his pay-off from Simon, which would come from the proceeds of the sale of his father-in-law's estate. Eventually.

On his arrival at Southampton and following a brief interview by the Hampshire police, Peter headed home. His calls to Annette's flat were unanswered, and her mobile number was obtainable. Before going to his house, he decided to drop in at the bookies, where he could kill two birds with one stone. He laughed aloud at his inappropriate thought and continued to think even more inappropriately about Annette.

"Sorry, mate," the helpful manager, Sid, replied to Peter's question, "she walked out on Friday, and we've not heard a word since. Funny though, you are about the tenth bloke that's enquired about her."

Sid's last words were left trailing as Peter flew out the door, running to his car. He didn't even place a bet. There was no response from his persistent pressing on the bell to Annette's flat, with the exception of a window on the ground floor being pushed open by an elderly, toothless man who volunteered the fact that "the tart upstairs has gone." As had most of Peter's (and his late wife's) possessions, which he would find out later.

Just as the ship was sailing down the Solent, Annette had been bedding her last victim—Alex Derwent. His keys even had his address on an attached tag, not that it would have mattered, because she knew that by the end of their third meeting she would have extracted his address from him. She had never failed. Annette always did her homework first: big gamblers, married, not younger than forty, and having had a vasectomy. For a good Catholic girl like Annette, that was important. If they were well endowed and accomplished lovers, it was a bonus. Annette liked bonuses. With Alex, she had a *big* bonus. This was her fourth meeting with Alex, and she had grown to enjoy her time with him. It didn't seem like business with Alex.

On seeing the bottle of *Casillero del Diablo,* Alex congratulated her. "An excellent wine you have there, love," he announced admiringly as he slipped on his shoes. "That's my favourite brand—the merlot, the sauvignon blanc, and the shiraz."

"Take it," Annette replied. "If you like it, take it. Wine doesn't float my boat anyway."

Alex smiled in gratitude; in gratitude for the wine and for Annette's warm and loving attentions. He rose to kiss her. Other things rose too, including his blood pressure as he noticed the time. Almost as an afterthought, Alex grabbed the bottle as Annette bid him a good night and expressed her undying love for him.

Annette was good that way; she never mixed up their names or forgot what their sexual preferences were. She kept a file on each one and knew when they were available, what clothes they liked her to wear, how they liked her hair, what they drank and ate, and whether or not she had to fake an orgasm. Annette also kept a box with the copy keys in it, each with a coloured tag with the address written in neat capital letters and cross-referenced to their files, which she had numbered one to nine. She showered, washed her hair (washing Alex out of it too), and then sat in her favoured chair dressed in a white towelling robe wrapped tightly around her, her hair swathed in a matching towel. Her

The Devil's Cellar

nine files were neatly piled on the floor. To someone else in the room, the incessant tapping of the ballpoint pen on Annette's teeth would have been infuriating, but to her the rhythm was soothing and helped her focus her thoughts.

For two hours, Annette made notes, crossed them out, and then wrote more notes. She juggled the files around, opening them one at a time randomly, and then finally put a big tick all the way through the last page of her plan. She resorted the files into her order of action with dates and times and then, jubilantly, retracted the ballpoint and tossed the pen onto the pile of papers. Her preparation was done; she knew what she had to do next. Firstly, she had to move. She had been in the flat six months, just long enough to find all of her victims. Now, in accordance with her scheme, she needed to move on.

Annette and Tommy arrived at the semidetached house of their first victim in a white van, which had "South Eastern Carpets" printed in red on the side together with a mobile phone number and the helpful "We are at your service" liveried on the rear panels. Annette knocked on the door of the house, not expecting a reply. She was not disappointed and slipped the key into the lock to let herself in. The van was as close to the front door as possible, and Annette, wearing a woolly hat to disguise her blonde hair and loose overalls to hide her figure, went in and straight upstairs. Tommy stayed in the van. Annette always knew a good piece of jewellery when she saw it, and she was not disappointed as she rummaged through the drawers and cupboards in the main bedroom.

She filled a bag with rings, necklaces, watches, and bracelets, leaving two rings that were both inscribed "To my darling

Tricia." Annette knew from past experiences that gamblers invariably presented jewellery to their wives almost in the same way that a cat brings a bird to its master when it knows that it is not in favour. Despite her professionalism, she allowed her sentimentality to win when it came to personalised jewellery. According to the file, both mister and missus were at work every day—he to earn money to feed his gambling habit; she to feed and clothe them. Even so, Annette allowed no more than twenty minutes to fill their van, selectively. They weren't common thieves; they were experts at their profession. They only took untraceable items that could be easily sold on through their good friend, Faisal—"Faisal the Fence," who always gave them a good price prior to expertly dismantling each piece of jewellery and then re-creating a new masterpiece that, ultimately, found its way into High Street shops. No one in the trade could understand how *Faisal Manufacturing Jewellery Limited* could produce such fine, and reasonably priced, pieces. Neither could the buyer from the popular retailer. All they understood was their extra profit.

Within thirty minutes, Annette and Tommy were driving toward their lock-up garage, where they could unload, sort, and store the day's bounty.

Annette and Tommy were partners. Partners in crime, not partners in bed. She had made, and enforced, the rule that her bedroom was out of bounds to Tommy. He reluctantly acceded. They cuddled rather than kissed. It was Annette's rules, and Tommy was happy to oblige—in return for food and lodging. And plenty of drink.

The next victim was scheduled for the next day at 11.15. The wife habitually went to visit her mother every Tuesday

The Devil's Cellar

and would leave at 11.00. Tommy and Annette arrived at the large detached house at 10.45, sat, and watched. *So that's what she looks like*, Annette thought to herself fifteen minutes later, as the other half of the second victim drove her small Fiat through the open gates and onto the road. The magnetic signs on the side of the van proclaiming to be "South Eastern Carpets" had been replaced with "One Two Three Plumbers". As soon as the car was out of sight, Annette manoeuvred the van into the drive and parked it where the Fiat had been less than two minutes earlier.

When they arrived at their third victim's house in the middle of the afternoon in their van, now liveried with "Wallington Joinery and Carpentry", Annette nearly decided to abandon the job as it was on a busy street with pedestrians and traffic buzzing around. "What do you think, Tommy?" she enquired. As Tommy's response was noncommittal, Annette reversed the van into the drive and went through the usual procedures. In less than fifteen minutes, they were on their way with the black holdall filled.

Something was bothering Annette, but she didn't know what it was.

The remaining six burglaries went as smoothly, and as lucratively, as expected. After the final theft, Annette removed the magnetic van signs and drove straight back to her flat. She brought down suitcases, clothes carriers, and boxes containing the entire moveable contents of their flat. They had perfected their timing, always moving after their last job. The new flat was not as nice, and Tommy was less than impressed with his quarters, but it would be suitably convenient until they were ready to consider the location for their next batch of burglaries.

Detective Sergeant Paul Roberts was put in charge of the pile of cases, which grew day by day. The police computer readily yielded five previous series of burglaries around the county—all unsolved. Each batch had a similar *modus operandi:* all within a five-mile radius, no forced entry, high value jewellery taken, white tradesman's van seen in the area, and between seven and ten break-ins carried out within a three-week period. DS Roberts visited and revisited the victims, trying to elicit the one clue that would solve the crimes. Fingerprints yielded nothing; neither did anyone notice anything out of the ordinary except a white van whose registration number remained a tightly guarded secret.

By the end of the following week, after they had completed their series of planned thefts, Annette called Faisal. She knew the ritual. He would offer her an amount; she would ask for treble; they would agree on double. Double in this case was £20,000. Without too much trouble, Faisal would sell the melted and remade jewellery to the retailers for £100,000, and they, in turn, would sell it to the public for £500,000.

DS Roberts and his assistant, DC Rowland, called on victim number four for the fifth time. A resigned wife ushered them in and invited them to sit on the settee. Paul ran through the events once more, neither spouse being able to add anything to what was already known. It was Roger Rowland who noticed. "You like a bet, then, sir?" he said, pointing to the *Racing Post* that was laid over the arm of a chair. The wife clicked her tongue on her teeth as her husband shuffled uneasily in his seat. "Well, yes," he replied, "but only the odd flutter." The wife clicked her tongue again, this time louder, and looked directly at her other half.

"And where do you go to bet, sir?" Roger added almost casually, throwing a knowing glance at his sergeant as they waited for the reply, which was just that fraction slow in coming. When it did it, was accompanied by a noticeable flush of his cheeks and a few beads of sweat on his brow.

The unmarked police car pulled up outside *Bet2Win* on the High Street and was pounced on by a parking warden almost before the engine stopped. On seeing the warrant card, the warden skulked away. Inside the bookies, Sid, the manager, was bemused by Roger's and Paul's questioning, and although he answered to the best of his abilities, he struggled to understand the line of inquiry. Neither officer was prepared to explain that all nine victims of the thefts in the area were customers at his branch because, at this stage, Sid was a suspect. The suspicion lifted as Sid gave his plausible and confirmable alibis for most of the burglaries. The detectives prodded and probed Sid's mind until Annette's name came floating out.

Roger patted his jacket pocket triumphantly as he left the magistrates complete with a search warrant for "the premises known as Flat 9, 15 Marlborough Court." Three police cars simultaneously pulled up outside of the block and, as the occupants of the vehicles ran to the front door, at least six pairs of curtains twitched. The tradesman's buzzer let them into the stairway, and ten pairs of feet ran up the two flights to number 9. "If you're looking for the tart, she's gone," the man on the ground floor volunteered to anyone who wanted to listen.

She had indeed gone. The cupboards, drawers, and shelves yielded nothing; the mail on the floor was only circulars and utility bills addressed "To the occupier." There was nothing;

nothing at all—except a pen, with *Bet2Win* embossed on the side, on the floor behind an open door. DS Roberts slipped the pen effortlessly into an evidence bag. He took one final look around the flat before dismissing his team. Roger and Paul systematically began to interview all of the neighbours, including the man who had noticed that "the tart had gone" and who gave them the number of the managing agent.

The nervous agent arrived, shortly after Paul had called him, together with his ex-tenant's file; he was horrified to see that the front door had been broken open. "Don't worry, sir," Paul said, "the carpenter is on his way." The tenant's file had little to offer. The application form, signed by Annette, was almost incomplete with just a name, Annette Smith, and a phone number which proved to be unobtainable. The description given by the agent matched perfectly with that which had been given by Sid and confirmed by most of the neighbours. The agent told them that Ms Smith had paid for the full period of the six months' tenancy and deposit in cash and had given him "a little extra." The little extra, it transpired, was what Annette was good at and involved the new double bed.

Back at the station, DS Roberts reported to his inspector. A picture of the mysterious Ms Smith was produced, together with her description, and the two officers retraced their steps to the nine victims. None of the wives knew the woman in the picture; none of the men, except Peter, admitted that they knew her—but Roger Rowland was perceptive. "Something a bit iffy here, guv; there's something that they're not telling us. Although she'd only been at the bookies for a few months, more than one of them must have seen her,

The Devil's Cellar

surely," he said as they sat back in the car. "How about if we got the blokes on their own?"

One by one, they admitted that they knew her. One by one, they admitted that they had had an affair with her. One by one, they admitted that they had mislaid their keys after seeing her.

"Well, that's it then; no doubt about it. All we've got to do now is find her!" DS Roberts exclaimed as he handed Annette's enhanced photo and description to Roger, with a dismissive wave of the hand, which DC Rowland knew to mean, "Put the information onto the Police National Computer."

It was two constables from the Cambridge police force who spotted her in the Lion Yard pedestrian precinct. Tommy was being aggressive, and Annette was helpless at calming him down. "Isn't that the one they are looking for in London?" the younger one asked.

The two constables looked at each other, both wanting to grab the tall buxom blonde-haired woman, neither of them wanting to deal with Tommy.

Will took charge of the situation. "Is everything all right, Miss ... erm ...?"

"Smith," she replied helpfully. Tommy had gone quiet and was sitting on his haunches, panting.

"Miss *Annette* Smith?" Will asked, but by more of a statement than a question. Her look said it all—she knew that they knew. Al called the dispatcher and arranged for a car and a van for the dog. By the time the three of them and the dog had reached the end of the shopping arcade, the vehicles had arrived in readiness to take the pair to the police station.

Roger Rowland took the call. "They've got her, guv—Cambridge."

DS Roberts and DC Rowland arrived at the Parkside Police Station in just under two hours in greater need of refreshments than to interview Annette Smith.

Annette waited in a cell, staring at a cup of tea, while Tommy was being treated to a bowl of food in the yard. Tommy was a pure white Japanese Akita dog, weighing almost seven stones, and when on his hind legs, he stood almost six foot tall. Some of the comers and goers in the yard took a detour around Tommy; others greeted and petted him as if they had known him forever.

She sat quietly in the interview room, with a solicitor by her side, awaiting the arrival of the officers from South London. Before Roger and Paul introduced themselves, Annette asked, in a demanding manner, what was going to happen to Tommy. The question remained unanswered until the preliminaries had been completed. "He will be taken to the RSPCA, unless you have a friend or relative who can look after him." Paul waited for her response.

"Tommy *is* my friend," Annette replied with tears forming in her eyes.

Annette was concerned; concerned for Tommy and concerned that she had missed her second period.

With the interview finished, she was taken back to the cells. "Can I see Tommy please?" she asked the female officer who was escorting her. "I just need to see him one last time. He's old, you know; I've had him for over twelve years." Her eyes became wet again, with some of her beauty disappearing with the mascara as it ran down her cheeks and onto Tommy's fur. The saliva on his tongue cleaned the remaining eye makeup off her face. As the door of the cell was being closed, Annette looked at the WPC with pleading in her eyes. "Excuse me, please, officer."

Yvonne Cutler paused and then pulled open the door again. Her facial expression encouraged Annette to continue. "I think I'm pregnant, I've missed two periods; I'm usually regular."

WPC Cutler helped Annette to the bench seat and sat down beside her.

"Can I get you anything? Do you want to see a doctor?" Annette shook her head vigorously. "Let me go and explain that to the detectives; ask for me if you need anything—all right?" Yvonne said as she stood up to leave, patting Annette gently on the shoulder.

Paul and Roger sat in the interview room and discussed their actions. First, they decided, they needed to get her back to London and then contact all the other areas where she had been active in order to ascertain how they wanted to proceed. Hopefully, they would let the South London team deal with her on behalf of them all. After all, none of the other constabularies had any ideas on the cases and had found no clues. WPC Cutler disturbed their conversation.

The journey back to London, which was unusually subdued, was interspersed with Annette saying, "He *will* be all right, won't he?" She meant Tommy; they assumed that she meant the baby. When she thought about her baby, she cried but they were tears of joy, not the tears of sadness that she felt for Tommy. Ever since the third burglary, something had been troubling Annette, but she hadn't been able to identify what it was. Annette was meticulous in her methodology—as soon as she had completed a job, she would destroy the file.

She couldn't remember number three, let alone what had struck the chord in her mind, yet something was bothering her. She was angry at whichever of her victims had lied to her. How *dare* they, she thought, how dare they lie to her. They all told her that they had had vasectomies.

Annette was charged with all forty-eight burglaries, to which she admitted, although she adamantly denied stealing certain items. Paul believed her; he knew from experience that victims would make false claims to their insurers and, thought Paul, why would she lie?

The judge sentenced her to three years, a light sentence in view of the help and assistance she had given to the police, including the name of her fence, Faisal. Annette was sent to *HMP Bronzefield,* which provided a family unit where she could look after her child for the first eighteen months. She had asked if there was an owner/dog prison—she missed Tommy.

In the pain of her labour, she remembered what had been bothering her. There had been a packet of contraceptive pills on the bedside table in the third house. "Who the hell was he?" she thought. The mother-and-baby liaison officer was there with her, holding her hand, and as the baby's head appeared, Annette screamed. She screamed in anguish more than in pain, "Where's Tommy? I need Tommy!"

The Devil's Cellar

The shouts of "It's a boy!" by the nurses were drowned out by the first cries of the baby. The child, wrapped in a towel, was laid in his mother's arms. Annette looked at him and realised who the father was.

She had had only one black lover, Alex.

As the baby was being born, the vet at the RSPCA was putting Tommy to sleep. No one wanted him; the devil had no need of a pet.

One Club Beats One Heart

"She reckons she gave the bottle to Alex Derwent. He's the managing director of *Polycom*, on the industrial estate on London Road." Jack Harvey didn't even look up. He waved his hand, dismissively, at his DS. "Get on with it, Terry."

"Come in!" Alex called in response to the knock on his office door. Ingrid opened it and walked nervously toward the light oak desk, behind which her boss was sitting in his high-backed leather chair, his elbows resting casually on its arms. He gestured to her to take a seat while he remained silent for a few moments; he watched Ingrid squirm uncomfortably on her chair. She had caused him to squirm enough times; time to seek redress, he mused. Alex sat forward suddenly, grabbed a handful of papers from his desk, and threw them at his soon-to-be-ex accounts manager. "Explain!" he shouted. "Explain!"

Ingrid was shaking. Even though she had not caused the errors, it was her responsibility, and she knew it. "I am terribly sorry, sir. I have dismissed the girl who did it. She was new—my fault, I didn't fully explain the procedures to her."

Alex reached for his pocket and took out a small stainless steel pillbox, opened the lid, and popped a sugar-free mint under his tongue as if the sweet smell of his breath would make his words any less bitter. Ingrid's personnel file was in the centre of his otherwise clear desk. "I'll have your immediate resignation; pack your things and leave now." The file had shown two previous disciplinary issues, and although he knew that technically he hadn't dealt with the situation correctly, he was a gambler. He felt the odds were in his favour. Alex saw her face flush and the trace of tears in her eyes as she stood to leave. "We'll pay you for the current month," he said, relenting, and then he looked down at his desk as she left his office.

"Hi, Anthony, how you doing? Just confirming our game tomorrow night." Alex made the same calls to Julian and Sebastian. All confirmed and they all added that they were looking forward to it. Bridge was a new game to Alex, as was wine drinking and the love of the arts. At his time of life, forty-seven, he had decided to seek the finer things in life—bridge, ballet, opera, classical music, and golf had all found a space in his life, as had designer-branded clothes and expensive jewellery. And Annette.

The insurer's loss adjusters had agreed on the list of stolen items and instructed him to get the replacements from one of their recommended jewellers, as no cash would be paid. *Damn*, he thought, *what will I do with* two *Rolex watches?* Annette hadn't taken the watch or a half-a-dozen other pieces, but Alex, nevertheless, told the police, and the insurers, that they had been stolen along with everything else. He knew that Annette was spending some time in prison, and although she had caused him a difficult and embarrassing time following the theft, he still thought about her frequently and fondly.

He didn't know about his son. Yet.

Sophia was putting on her coat. "Can I take a bottle, dear?" she asked Alex.

"Hang on a moment; I'll get you one," he replied as he kneeled down and opened the wine cupboard. "Is a red okay?" he called back, holding the bottle of *Casillero del Diablo* that Annette had given him, the 2006 vintage, not one of his stock of 2007 merlots that he had bought by the caseload.

Again he smiled to himself at the thought of Annette and the cruel irony of giving the bottle to his wife. "See you later," he said. "Have a lovely evening."

"I may stay over, Alex, Vicky's feeling a bit down, and I am sure this won't be the only bottle we open." From the size of the bag she was carrying, he knew that she would be staying. He was right. In fact, she would stay three nights with her sister-in-law, her late brother's widow. Vicky was very down.

Just as he was ready to leave for work the following morning, the postman deposited a bundle of letters through the door. Alex gave them each a cursory glance: bill, bill, junk, junk … he paused as he saw the letter from HM Prison Service. The letter was from Annette and had a photograph enclosed. A photograph of a baby boy.

The Devil's Cellar

Anthony, Julian, and Seb arrived together. Julian was a nondrinker and collected the other two on his way over—he knew that they both enjoyed the nineteenth hole at the golf club where they were all members.

It was Sebastian who had taught them how to play bridge, although he often shook his head in disbelief at their slow development. For him it was second nature; for them it was a struggle, although they all felt that they had become quite proficient in the art of the game.

"So," said Alex as he ushered the trio into the lounge, where the green baize card table was set in the centre laden with two packs of *Waddington's Number 1* playing cards and four score pads with pencils, "what are we all drinking?"

"Do you have a tomato juice?" Julian asked tentatively, as if he wasn't aware that it was Alex's favourite non-alcoholic drink.

Seb went straight over to the drinks trolley, on which there was a ship's decanter with its bowl full of red wine. His eyes sparkled as he picked it up triumphantly. "Ah! So what wine is it this week? Something more challenging, I hope." For the five weeks that they had been playing cards, a contest had evolved. Seb was, so he claimed, able to identify any wine that Alex served. The first two weeks, the wager had been won by the host for modest bets of £50, but as the weeks progressed, the stake had become greater, and for each of the following three weeks, Seb had won. The three of them were awestruck at just how accurate Seb was at identifying not only the grape variety, but also the vineyard's location and the year of production. Each week Alex had tried to find a more obscure wine, and he was confident that he could outwit Seb; each week it was *he* who was outwitted. But not this week. This week he was certain that Sebastian would be humbled and humiliated.

Alex wasn't in the mood for the wager that evening; the disquieting news that he had received in the post that morning had unnerved him, but he was sure that fortune would turn his way. Seb took a clear wine glass from the shelf under the trolley and held up the goblet to check on its cleanliness, and then he sniffed it to ensure that it had not been contaminated by another wine. He clicked his fingers impatiently at Alex. "Candle, where's the candle? How can I be expected …?"

His habitual rudeness and usual arrogance hadn't gone unnoticed by both Julian and Anthony, who exchanged knowing glances before engaging in a nervous trivial conversation in an attempt to brush aside Seb's petulance. Alex skulked off, returning with a lit candle on a glass base. "I can't use a *scented* candle, now, can I?" Seb almost screamed at Alex, who admitted that he had "things" on his mind. "I'm going outside for a smoke. Get me a *proper* candle."

Each week the evening had become more tense; each week Seb had become less tolerable and less likeable. But he was the captain of the golf club and owner of a large chain of shoe shops, and everyone *had* to like the captain. The front door was left ajar and the click of Seb's lighter could be heard, followed by a cough that was, undoubtedly, the result of the first draw on his cigar. Julian and Anthony continued their conversation whilst Alex scurried in and out of the lounge, seemingly preoccupied, but looking and listening. Finally, he heard the security light switch click and the halogen bulb illuminate the side path and bin store. He also

The Devil's Cellar

heard the lid of the bin being opened, then a few seconds later being closed. Alex smiled.

Seb smiled too, as he looked in the bin. Then he saw the letter.

Alex returned to the lounge carrying the unscented candle, putting it on the trolley to await Seb's approval. Julian and Anthony sat themselves down at the card table, opposite each other, and each picked up a fresh pack of cards, breaking the seals, removing the jokers, and then shuffling them thoroughly in anticipation of the start of the game.

"Your drinks!" Alex exclaimed. "So sorry." He walked over to the trolley, pouring the tomato juice for Julian and a beer for Anthony. He carried them over to his guests, together with the sealed envelope that contained the details of the decanted wine. Alex placed the envelope between the two of them, waiting for one of them to take it for safekeeping. Julian leaned forward, picked up the envelope, and slipped it into his jacket pocket. "This one he will not get; I am sure of that. Anyone want a side bet?" Both of them looked into their glasses, mumbling negatives.

Seb came in and walked straight over to the drinks trolley, poured some of the wine into the glass, and held it at arm's length in front of the glowing candle. The smell of the cigar lingered on his clothes and on his breath, and although Julian was a non-drinker, he wondered how anyone could taste anything with the taint of tobacco in his mouth.

"And what's the bet this week, old boy?" Seb said challengingly "£500?" Simultaneously, Julian and Anthony gasped.

"Let's make it interesting, eh Seb? How about £1,000?" Alex responded brazenly.

"What do you say to £5,000, old boy?"

"Steady on, guys, we're here to play bridge," ventured Anthony.

"Shut up," sneered Seb, directing his reply at Anthony, but still staring at Alex. "Well, do we have a bet or not?"

By way of an acceptance, Alex leaned forward and extended his right hand to Seb.

Seb took a gulp of wine and chewed on it for a moment before allowing it to flow down his throat. He voiced a "humph," not wishing to commit himself, and took the remaining seat at the table opposite Alex. The atmosphere was tense and as Anthony dealt the cards, Seb began to preach to them whilst continuing to savour the wine. "Remember, no-trumps beats everything; spades beats the other suits; hearts beats diamonds and clubs; and clubs is at the bottom of the ranking." All three looked at each other and either raised their eyes to heaven or shook their heads in disbelief. They had mastered, at least, the fundamentals of the bidding part of the game. All four sat in quiet contemplation, sorting and evaluating their hands. Anthony looked up, paused, and then hesitantly proclaimed, "Two hearts."

"Two hearts? Are you sure? You *do* know what that means, don't you?"

"Yes, Seb, I do," Anthony replied.

"A taste of cherry …"

"Eh?" Julian said quizzically.

"The wine, the wine—berries and currants," Seb blustered as he glared at Anthony. "Well, what have you got in your hand to merit a two hearts bid?"

"Nineteen points; a five-card heart suit; two honours, king high."

Seb took another gulp, wincing slightly as the acidity hit his throat. "Plumy, with a hint of mocha ... No! That is a bid of two *clubs*—your partner with six to ten points would bid two hearts." Seb's manner lightened a little as he noticed Alex's shoulders drop slightly and a hint of resignation appeared in his eyes. Seb passed on his bid and leaned back to reach out for the decanter. Julian, having been prompted by Seb during his rant, triumphantly bid two hearts; Alex followed his partner's lead and passed. Anthony remembered the response "Two no-trump" and glared challengingly at Seb, who was refilling his glass, seemingly oblivious to the bidding. Sebastian was attempting to keep a straight face as he watched Alex whilst he, in turn, was secretly enjoying himself at seeing Seb get more and more intoxicated and ready to fall into the trap.

"Three spades," Julian responded with a smile, but his self-belief was shattered as Seb threw him a hostile glance accompanied by "What did you say?"

Julian racked his brain: respond to two no-trump with your best suit; he was sure that it was the correct bid. "Three spades," Julian reiterated.

Seb glared at him. "Toasty oak. Yes; correct bid." Four spades was called, which Anthony played impeccably, winning the ten tricks needed for the game.

By the end of the first rubber, won by Julian and Anthony, Seb had finished the decanter. He slammed the glass on the table, sat back, and hung one arm over the chair-back, with a grin that screamed victory.

"Well," asked Alex, "do you know what you have been drinking?"

Sebastian's eyes were glazed and his tongue protruding slightly from his half-open mouth, his chin resting on his chest.

"Tell you what," he said. "How about making it *really* interesting. My car for your car."

"Steady on," Julian interjected. "This is stupid."

Seb swivelled on his chair to face Julian, poking his forefinger toward his face. "I am not talking to *you*; you shut the fuck up."

Anthony stood, ready to protest violently. "And you," Seb shouted at Anthony, "you sit down!"

Alex remained calm. "Your new Mercedes coupé for my three-year-old Peugeot coupé. Is that right?"

Seb stood up, slightly unsteadily, extending his open hand toward Alex.

"There are two witnesses here, Seb. Once more. Are you sure?"

Seb's hand remained outstretched toward Alex, who grasped it with both of his. "Okay, Seb, what do you think you have been drinking?"

Sebastian stayed standing. "A Chilean merlot, central region. I would say a 2007 vintage. Am I right?"

Alex remained relaxed and gesticulated to Julian to open the envelope that had been in his pocket all evening. He leaned forward and slowly opened it.

"Get on with it, will you," Seb slurred impatiently.

In a pique, Julian lowered the opened envelope to the table, watching Seb's anger mount, and just as Seb leaned across to grab the envelope, Julian picked it up again and pulled out the cream sheet of paper. "Just for clarification, Seb, you said a Chilean merlot, central region. 2007 vintage. Correct?"

"Yes, yes. Just get on with it, will you!" Seb shrieked.

Julian was enjoying the event; Alex seemed unfazed; Anthony remained a bewildered onlooker. "Well, it *was* a 2007 Chilean wine, and yes, it *was* from the central region, but it was a cabernet sauvignon, *not* a merlot."

"You are a liar!" Sebastian screamed, his face red with rage. "I *saw* the bottle in the bin with my own eyes."

Anthony's jaw dropped; Julian just stared at Seb, shaking his head from side to side in disbelief; Alex smirked. Sebastian realised what he had just said. He had let the cat out of the bag. He deliberately knocked over both his chair and the card table with his fists tightly clenched, shaking uncontrollably with anger. "The bottle, if you wish to see it, is behind the trolley. I will leave it to you to notify the DVLA. Drop the keys off in the morning will you, *old boy?*" Alex added the "old boy" with a flourish as Seb ran toward the door.

"I've not finished with you three yet," Seb screeched, "especially you, you, you black bastard."

"A true gent," Anthony said sarcastically, as the three of them started to clear up the havoc left by the captain of their golf club.

Mid-morning on the next day, Saturday, the doorbell rang. Seb followed Alex into the lounge, where Alex had been relaxing in an armchair, reading the morning paper. There were no pleasantries. He held out his hand, ready to receive Seb's car keys. Sebastian stood in front of Alex, arms akimbo. "And just who is this Annette woman?" he said, holding out the wet, stained, yet intact, letter from *HMP Bronzefield* that he had retrieved from the refuse bin the previous night. "The letter in return for calling off the bet."

Alex grabbed the letter and stuffed it into his trouser pocket as he said, in a controlled voice, "Now get out."

Alex, Julian, and Anthony were sitting in a quiet corner of the club's lounge, in deep conversation, sharing a large cafetière of dark roast coffee and a selection of Danish pastries.

Anthony saw Seb come into the room and greet the players standing at the bar. Three large whiskeys later, he walked purposefully, though slightly unsteadily, across the room to where the three of them were sitting. "Sorry about Friday evening, lads. I was having a hard day. All forgiven?"

Julian and Anthony looked toward Alex for guidance.

"Sure," he said coldly as he stood, followed by the other two, and shook Sebastian's hand.

The captain led them out to the first tee, followed by Alex, with the other two dragging behind in deep conversation, looking at the two in front as they spoke. Anthony's tee shot was straight and safe, and they all followed with similar shots, culminating with them all scoring four on the par four hole. The mood lightened slowly as they walked to the second tee, and by the time they had reached the eighth green, the conversation reverted to its normal good nature. The same could not be said for the weather, as the sky darkened, the winds gathered pace, and the rain cascaded down on the four hapless golfers. Their umbrellas were useless against the torrential downpour, and Seb was struggling to light his cigar.

"Forget the smoke, Seb, have a swig of this," Anthony said as he removed a silver hip flask from his golf bag and passed it to Sebastian. They watched intently as Seb swallowed mouthful after mouthful of Anthony's cognac brandy until the flask was empty. Without a word of thanks or apology, he handed the flask back as Alex and Julian, who were standing behind Seb, grinned and winked at each other.

"Well, it's eased; shall we carry on?" Julian asked, "We are at the ninth, and it seems to be clearing." They walked the short distance to the muddy and waterlogged tee with Seb ambling along behind them, the effect of the alcohol taking hold. Anthony, who was the only left-hander, bent down to put his ball on the peg.

"I go first, I think; *I* won the last hole," Seb said challengingly.

The other three readied themselves for the moment that they had long rehearsed.

Seb leaned forward to remove Anthony's ball and replace it with his own. As he did so, Julian hooked his foot around Seb's leg, pulling him off-balance and causing Seb to topple face down onto the mud. Alex grabbed Seb's golf bag and threw it over the prone body. In a state of shock, Sebastian tried to push off the heavy golf bag and attempted to get up. Alex put his foot down hard on the bag, pinning the dazed captain to the ground while Anthony, gripping his club, poised himself for the tee shot. There was no ball. Just Sebastian's head. The club swung through the air in a perfect arc and made contact with Seb's skull with a satisfying crack.

Anthony stood over Seb's body just as his heart completed its last beat and said in a clear, strong voice, "Please don't be rude to my friends, it's not nice." It had all gone exactly according to plan. Alex removed the bag while Julian telephoned the clubhouse. "There has been a terrible accident on the ninth tee. The chairman seems to have accidentally killed the captain. Call 999, will you?"

The devil smiled. He needed a fourth player for bridge.

Unconditional Love

"Forensics have found something, guv."

Jack Harvey groaned and cocked his head to one side, waiting for his sergeant's words.

"They've reconstructed the bottle as best they could and found a thumb print on its neck."

Jack's eyes rolled heavenward. He was weary with the false dawns of hope that his team kept bringing him.

"The thumb print was upside down, guv, as if the bottle was held upside down," Terry explained, imitating the motion with his left hand, "and … there was a trace of blood. But *not* the victim's blood. It *has* to be the murderer's."

"So, Terry, pray tell me, just *who's* thumb print and blood is it?"

No sooner had Sophia rang on the bell, than the door was pulled open by Vicky, who fell into her arms, her whole body shuddering with the release of her tears. Sophia's hands were full, one with the bottle of *Casillero del Diablo* and the other with her bulky overnight case. She hurriedly broke away, guided Vicky back into her hallway, unloaded her luggage and wrapped both arms around her swaying gently from side to side, rubbing her back as a mother would do to her baby. Sophia could feel the torrent of Vicky's tears running down her neck. Slowly the tears abated and Vicky's grip loosened. Sophia let her arms drop as she said in a soft voice, "Go and sit inside, I'll make us a nice cup of tea."

By the time the tea was ready, Vicky had composed herself, although the red eyes and sore nose, as well as the unbrushed hair, were the clues to her condition.

"I can't do it no more, Soph, I really can't." Vicky couldn't stop the tears as they resumed the race to her chin via her cheeks. "I've had it with him. I can't go on."

"Tell me, sweet, tell me everything."

Vicky began to describe to her sister-in-law just how her father had begun to deteriorate. "It started one day when I was taking him breakfast. He asked me what day it was. I told him. He said, 'Thanks, Joan'." Vicky took out her soggy handkerchief and wiped her face. "That was my Mum's name, you know. I didn't think any more of it until a few months later, when I saw him nip in and out of the loo a few times—I assumed he was having trouble with his waterworks. Then I noticed he wasn't taking his pills. 'I forgot,' he said when I asked him. Then he put his watch on the wrong wrist. I should have spotted it earlier, you know, but my mind has been on poor Nigel. It's been nearly two years since he went, Soph, two years." They both sat in quiet contemplation for a minute; Vicky in remembrance of her husband and Sophia in remembrance of her elder brother.

It was Vicky who broke the silence. "And we get into terrible arguments, Soph. He talks about the roses in the garden and the little pond. He had them when he was a child. Him and Mum lived in a flat, and we don't have a pond here. So I took him to the doctor. She asked him questions. When he said that he had been a boxer, the doc raised her eyebrows and wrote a bit. Then she asked him to sit outside and wait. She told me she thinks he may have dementia and that she wanted to send him for tests. Then there was a scream and some shouting from the waiting room. We both went outside. Dad had clenched fists and was standing by an old man with a bloody lip who was being helped to his feet. A lady said that a child had been playing in the play area and rang a bell. She said for no reason at all, Dad got up and punched the man. The police came. Oh, goodness, it was awful, Soph, really awful."

"What's the significance? Am I missing something?" asked Sophia.

"You remember, don't you, Dad was a boxer. He won a gold medal in the Tokyo Olympics. *Southpaw Sammy*, they called him. He's left handed, you know. He heard the bell and was ready for the next round." Vicky reached to the sideboard, picked up a photo of a young, handsome man in boxing shorts and gloves, with an Olympic gold medal hanging around his neck.

The door opened and a tired-looking old man shuffled into the room. "Dad, you remember Sophia, don't you?"

He turned and stared at Sophia. "Who are you? I don't know you."

He then turned to look at Vicky. Sophia would not have recognised Sam. The last time she saw him was at her brother's funeral. Sam had looked strong and fit and as handsome as he was in the photo. And that was, she reminisced, only two years ago.

"We will have lunch soon, Dad. Anything special you want?"

"Ice cream, I want ice cream. When are we going to see the ice-cream man?" and with that, Sam wandered off toward the door.

"See what I mean? The doctors in their white coats are ice-cream men to him. When they put that wooden thingy in his mouth, he bites down on it and licks it like it was a lolly stick."

"Is he ever lucid?"

"Sometimes, but rarely. And it's hard to know when he's in this world, but I have begun to notice a pattern. He goes all still, doesn't move, and then looks at me and calls my name and says something sensible. But it only lasts maybe a minute at the most and not very often at that."

They sat in silence as Sophia began to in take the enormity of Vicky's responsibilities.

"I love him, Soph, unconditionally. I must look after him, I *must*."

Lunch was a simple meal of tomato soup (his favourite,

said Vicky) and Welsh rarebit. Sam slurped the soup off the spoon, which he held in his clenched fist, and if it wasn't for the napkin that was tied around his neck, he would have had the contents of a quarter of a can of *Heinz 57* all down his jumper. Sam spat out his first mouthful of his Welsh rarebit. "It's hot. I don't want it. Can I go and play, Mum?" Sam got up, with the napkin still tied around his neck, and went into the hallway. He sat on the floor with his toy lorry, holding it upside down and spinning the wheels with his fingers.

"He will spend hours doing that, then he'll throw it at me, saying, 'It's broken. I want Daddy to mend it.' It upsets me so much, Sophia, and it's getting worse by the hour. But I won't let him go into a care home. He's my Dad."

The two of them went back into the lounge and continued talking for the rest of the afternoon, although Sophia was finding it hard to come to terms with Sam's condition and was finding it even harder to offer any advice to her sister-in-law. Vicky's mood was slowly lightening, and she even managed a giggle at an anecdote told by Sophia. "First time I've laughed for ages. Thank you, Soph, you are an angel."

Sam shuffled into the room, and as expected, he threw his toy at Vicky, demanding it be mended, and sat down in the brown leather club chair that had become his sanctuary.

"Do you want a little sleep, Dad? You must be tired. You've had a busy day."

"Why do you call me Dad? I want my Mummy to put me to bed," Sam said, looking straight at Sophia. Vicky looked at Sophia, her eyes pleading. Sophia stood and walked over to Sam.

"Just lay him on the bed, Soph, and put the duvet over him." Sophia took his hand and led him upstairs. When she returned, she noticed that Vicky had started crying again. "The other day, I'd been shopping; as I opened the door, Dad was standing there. He started screaming at me, 'There's an angry old man over there. He's got his fist tight. He's angry; he's pointing at me. He's shouting at me! Mummy, tell him to go away.' He grabbed my wrist and pulled me into the back room. He was really agitated, shaking. He pointed at the window. It was dark outside, and he could see our reflections. 'See, there he is! And he's got *his* mum.' I pulled the curtains closed, led him to his chair, and brought him a glass of warm milk. He soon calmed down."

It was Sophia's turn to cry and Vicky's turn to comfort her.

"Is he a danger to himself or anyone else?" Sophia asked.

"I asked the same question of the doctor. She couldn't or wouldn't answer. All he said was to lock dangerous thing away, especially pills and knives. Sometimes he goes wandering. Often stays in the garden—I caught him eating worms the other day—but occasionally he wanders off down the road. He shadow-boxes, still thinks he is in his prime. Someone always brings him back; I put a name and address tag on the back of his jumper. He doesn't know it's there, so he can't take it off."

"So, what are we going to do, love? How can Alex and I help? I mean *really* help. I hadn't realised just how bad things were."

"I need my life, Sophia; I lost a chunk when Nigel died. But he's my Dad."

"Look, let us help you. I am sure we can find somewhere for him to have a few days holiday. There must be somewhere that does that."

"There are places, but they are expensive. I can't afford …"

Sophia interrupted, "Hush, Alex and I will sort all that out and I'm sure that your brother will help too."

Vicky's tears were curtailed by Sam shuffling into the room. "My bed is wet, really wet." The evidence was there. The dark staining on Sam's trousers was spreading slowly down his legs.

Sophia busied herself in the kitchen preparing supper whilst Vicky took Sam back upstairs. She came down with a bundle of bed linen and clothes, which she stuffed into the washing machine. Without the question being asked, Vicky said, "Once or twice a night. Sometimes in the day too."

After Vicky fed Sam and put him to bed, she said, "This is the only time I get. I never know what the next day will bring." They sat chatting, trying to avoid the topic of Sam, until after midnight.

Sophia heard the night-time routine, but only once.

Vicky fed Sam his porridge, into which she had crushed his pills; she had found that this was the easiest way to ensure that he took his medication. After breakfast, Sam went into the lounge and sat in his club chair as Vicky turned on the television for him, handed him the remote control, and showed him, yet again, how to change the programmes. He liked cartoons and sat quietly for an hour watching the never-ending stream of animated films of dogs chasing cats and cats chasing mice.

"Last month he came into the kitchen, *really* frantic. It was just before lunch; he was flapping his arms. 'Where's the stars? I need the stars, where's the stars?' I tried rationalising with him. 'It's not night-time yet, the sun is still out. There are no stars till it's bedtime.' He wouldn't relax. He got more and more annoyed and bewildered. I couldn't pacify him. I tried to make him take another tranquiliser, but he spat it at me. Then all of a sudden, he stood still. 'Stars,' he said, 'stars, stars … stairs! Where are the stairs?' I'm scared, Sophia, really scared."

They heard Sam close the back door as he went into the garden. "I can't keep him prisoner, can I, Sophia? He has to have some freedom. He goes out the front sometimes."

Sophia nodded sympathetically and tried to guide the conversation away from Sam. She understood how her sister-in-law felt and was worried about *her* state of mind.

"Let's go to the shops, Vicky. We can do a bit of feel-good shopping. What do you say? We can take Sam."

Vicky went to the back door. "Do you want a ride in Sophia's car? We are going to the shops."

"No, I am tired. I want bed. Bring me sweets."

"We can't leave him, Soph."

"He will be fine in bed. An hour at the most, eh? We need a little time out, don't we? You told me that you go to the shops on your own. We'll get some things for tea and open that bottle of wine. We should have been on our third bottle by now. Never had a bottle stay unopened for so long. What do you say?" As she blustered, Sophia ushered Vicky through the front door, almost knocking over the bottle that still took centre stage on the hall table.

Laden with bags, Sophia and Vicky arrived back home two hours later. Sophia noticed that the bottle of *Casillero del Diablo* was gone. Vicky called out to Sam, "We are back with sweeties for you." There was no response. She ran upstairs, calling out to her father. There was no reply. Panicking, Vicky ran from room to room. "Soph, he's gone!"

Sophia checked the garden but the back door was locked on the inside. The two women met at the bottom of the stairs, the colour drained from both their faces. There was no sign of Sam.

"We'll give it twenty minutes. If he doesn't come back on his own, we will start looking. Okay? Come on, sit down, love, I'll make us some tea." Sophia remained rational; Vicky started crying. "Does your Dad drink?"

"I give him a brandy every now and then but he likes lemonade or milk. Why do you ask?"

"The bottle of wine is gone, Vicky."

"It's on the hall table, Soph, where you left it."

"It was there when we went out; I almost knocked it over."

"He wouldn't drink the wine. I wonder where it is."

Vicky's tears stopped and she reached for her handbag and rummaged in it until she found her lipstick.

Sophia marvelled at the amazing powers of tea, as they both sat cradling their cups.

The bell rang. They jumped up together and raced each other to the front door.

"I found him wandering, so I brought him back," the kindly neighbour said as she released her grip on Sam's arm, guiding him in through the door.

"Oh thanks, Marge, where was he? We've been so worried; we were just going to call the police."

"He was up in Sussex Avenue; loads of police there, flashing lights and everything; quite a commotion up there. Your Dad had been watching," Marge replied as she acknowledged Vicky's thanks once again and walked back along the path.

"Where have you been, you naughty boy, you?" Vicky half-heartedly chastised her father as she closed the door. "And you stink of alcohol! Did you take the bottle of wine that Sophia brought? Did you drink it? Oh! You are bleeding from your hand. And your shirt is wet and stained too. You must be cold; I'll run a bath for you."

Sam looked up at her. "Who are you? Do I know you? You are a kind lady. Have you seen my Mum? I need to tell her something."

"No dear, I haven't seen her. What do you need to tell her?"

Sam looked at his daughter. "Tell who? What?" he said with the usual vague look in his eyes.

Vicky led him up the stairs toward the bathroom and began to take off his clothes. Even though she had been helping him undress for some months, she still felt embarrassed doing it and seeing her father naked. She helped him step into the bath and lowered him into the warm water, placing his hands on the rails on either side, and then gathered his stained and wet clothes. As she opened the lid of the laundry bin in the hall, she heard her father call, "Vicky, Vicky, are you there?"

"Yes, Dad, I'm here," she called back realising that it was a lucid moment; praying that it would last; knowing that it wouldn't. She walked the few steps to the bathroom door. Sam looked up at her. Almost imperceptibly, his face began to twitch as if every facial nerve was gathering enough strength to pull a memory from the depths of his brain.

"I *told* him to get out of my chair," he said. "He was sitting in *my* chair. He wouldn't. So I thought I would give him the bottle. He wouldn't take it. It broke on his head. He didn't move." Sam turned his head toward the taps in front of him.

"Where's my Mum? I want my Mum."

Tess and I were sitting on the sofa watching a re-run of *"Notting Hill"* on the television, with her head resting on my shoulder and her soft hair tickling my chin. She sighed as I gently brushed it aside. I looked at my watch and smiled inwardly at the thought of an early night with my wife. The phone rang and Tess sat up in a way that indicated that it was me that should quieten its shrill.

"Hello", I answered, with a slight question in my tone.

"Victor?" came the reply "It's me Victoria."

I understood why our parents had perversely named me Victor and my twin sister Victoria. We were born on the day of dad's victory at the Tokyo Olympics. I hadn't seen Vicky or dad since Tess and I got married. Vicky bore all of the burden of dealing with our dad and I felt guilty. I made a mental note to rectify the situation.

"How are you sis? How's dad?"

There was no reply, just sobbing. Vicky quickly composed herself before she said:

"Victor… Victor… I think dad's killed someone."

Epilogue

The devil sat in his cellar, humming to himself. He was pleased with the words that he had written:

> I've been around for thousands of years
> Heard all the laughter and seen all the tears.
> I invented that Faustian thing.
> I am wed to the world for the trouble I bring.
> My mission here is to cheat and confuse,
> Fought many battles with Muslims, Christians, and Jews.
> You can see the smile on my face
> As I take you down to that fiery place.
> This world is full of tragic events
> Given to you to help you repent.
> If I was you, I'd laugh in my face.
> I only exist if you give me the space

(Lyrics from the song "Trouble" reproduced with the kind permission of Brian Shaw)